Espoused

JEAN MARIE DAVIS

Espoused
Published by Wren Park Publishing
Centerport, NY

ISBN: 978-0-578-49746-4
FICTION / Humorous

Cover and Interior design by Victoria Wolf, wolfdesignandmarketing.com

Wren Park
PUBLISHING

For my Mom
Rosemary "Tish" Meehan
Who loved to read
And taught me to love it too.

"In every marriage more than a week old, there are grounds for divorce. The trick is to find and continue to find grounds for marriage."

— Robert Anderson

CHAPTER 1

The First Appointment

SOMETIMES FIGHTING FOR LOVE seemed like folly.

Especially late in the afternoon when all Gwen Stevens had seen in her Long Island home office were star-crossed lovers willing to throw caution and sanity to the wind.

Gwen straightened her pantsuit, fluffed the bow on her blouse, then blotted her shiny cocoa skin with a tissue, making sure her black modest bun still hugged the top of her head. She shelved the files from her morning cases, clearing a spot on her small oak desk, and arranged the sparse remaining items: her line of Parker pens, a paperweight, and the GWENDOLYN STEVENS Esq. nameplate. A family photo—taken at her son Terrell's graduation from law school—sat on the right side of her desk. Taking a breath, she looked at the smiling faces of her family, reminding her that, as dirty as the business of espousing was, she was doing some good in this world.

After all, some people just belonged together.

The doorbell rang. Gwen glanced at the clock. Three p.m. exactly. Even if these clients were a couple of lovesick puppies, at least they had punctuality going for them.

She didn't like to disturb her husband by letting the doorbell ring more than once. Trim and spry for nearly sixty, she jogged past the closed door to what was once the living room, but now her husband's sick room, and made it to the foyer just before the doorbell rang again.

She opened the door to her latest appointment: The Healys.

Gwen had only taken down the basics when she booked the appointment: Sara and Thomas Healy lived in the town of Greenlawn, a suburb on the north shore of Long Island. The village was part of a larger township known as Huntington, which was a fifty-minute train trip into New York City, where many residents worked Monday through Friday. Sara and Tom had been married fourteen years and had two children, Samuel and Avery, ages eleven and fourteen. That was all she ever asked for, and yet even that was not necessary. All couples Gwen dealt with were, essentially, the same: middle-aged, married anywhere between twelve and fourteen years, many with a child or two or three.

And always, always, always boasting the same smug expressions: strong, self-righteous smiles, as if their situation were wholly differ- ent from those of the hundreds of other couples she'd dealt with over the years.

Although they never *were* different.

"Hello, Mr. and Mrs. Healy," she said, shaking hands with a very pretty, very thin woman with shoulder-length hair pulled back in a ponytail, as well as the tall, handsome man standing beside her. She led them into the office and pointed out the two chairs across from her desk, each covered in blue pleather.

As the couple sat, she noticed all the telltale signs: the way Tom Healy pulled the chair out for Sara, making sure she was comfortable before sitting down himself. The way he positioned his chair closer to hers. The way Sara reached over and grabbed his hand. The way they smiled at each other adoringly, once they sat down, knees touching.

They were still in love.

And so, they had no choice. They had to seek out someone like Gwen. An espouse lawyer. Gwen had not always been an espouse lawyer. She had worked in a large, multi-national law firm in New York City as head of the firm's litigation section. Then Dennis had become sick and she needed, no, wanted, to work at home. Dennis, a very talented and respected espouse lawyer, was the one who suggested she take over his client list. She thought it was crazy at first, but they worked closely together, and Gwen picked it up. As Dennis needed more time to fight the cancer, Gwen picked up more and more of his work. Now, here she was, meeting with the Healys.

Tom cleared his throat. "Thank you for seeing ..."

Gwen held up a hand. Tom closed his mouth at once. Couples she met with were usually excited to get this over and done with, but it wasn't nearly as simple or quick as they hoped. They always seemed so certain, until they learned the many hoops they would have to jump through to become espoused. She pulled out a pile of paperwork, the first of many steps they would need to take.

Sometimes, that was all a couple needed to rethink espouse.

"Before you say anything," Gwen said, "I'd like to let you know what you're in for. Getting espoused is not easy."

"Oh, we know," Sara said, patting her husband's knee gently. "We are fully prepared to undertake any of the necessary steps. It's that important to us."

From the khaki pants and Talbots cardigan sweater to the pony-tail pulled back in a black scrunchie, it was clear this woman was devoted to family. Stay-at-home mom, Gwen guessed. Tastefully simple? Talbots? Definitely not LuLaRoe, or she would be sporting obnoxiously printed leggings.

Gwen shifted her eyes from Sara to Tom, who nodded solemnly. She let out a breath, fighting her first instinct—she wanted to slap them both across the face and say, *Snap out of it!*

She didn't, of course.

She simply smiled back at them. "Well, since few of my clients ever understand what getting espoused actually means, please allow me to explain what it entails."

They both straightened and nodded. They might have thought their minds were made up, but Gwen always made an attempt to ensure they were both willing to follow the case to completion. It did not help for her to put in work only to find out that a couple wanted to uncouple after all.

"As you know, in the United States, all first marriages are automatically uncoupled after fifteen years. Fifteen years is considered the appropriate life cycle of a marriage. Prior to the official ending of your marriage, if both parties are in agreement, you may petition to become espoused, which is the reason for your visit today," Gwen recited in a monotone voice.

They both nodded eagerly.

"*However*," she said, biting off the word as she leaned back in her chair. "I always consult with my clients first, as I want to make sure you're fully informed of the process before you agree to the espouse proceedings."

Sara's voice was gentle but assured. "We've done our research, Mrs. Stevens. We're already prepared."

"Nevertheless," Gwen said, holding up a finger, "as your lawyer, it would be remiss of me not to go over the particulars. Many people considering espouse realize it's not for them once they hear of the many obstacles."

Tom removed his hand from the top of Sara's, which was still resting on his knee, and pushed his glasses higher up the bridge of his nose. "We won't decide that. We're fully committed."

Gwen inhaled sharply. *Fully committed. Oh, sure.* She wished she had a dollar for every time she'd heard that phrase.

"I'm sure you are, but *nevertheless,*" she said again, the final word pointed as if to say she was planning to continue regardless of any opposition they laid down.

"Mrs. Stevens, we didn't make this decision lightly. We know what we are up against. We came to you to start the espouse process. We want to stay together," he said sternly, grabbing Sara's hand and setting his jaw while looking directly at Gwen.

"Okay," Gwen said, "then let's go through some of this paperwork, shall we?"

Tom and Sara looked lovingly at one another and back at Gwen.

"Did you buy your second home using any federal government uncoupling escrow funds?" Gwen asked.

Tom nodded. "Yes, we bought a condo close to our current home for me to live in after the uncoupling. I spoke to our accountant, who told us to wait for the espouse decree before selling it and paying back the government with the funds from the sale."

Gwen noted this on her yellow pad. "How much of the government housing escrow did you match?"

Sara chimed in, "We matched the full $15,000 a year allowable by law. The accountant already explained we will have to pay back taxes and a penalty on the matched funds since it was tax-deductible."

Usually, once potential clients thought through this part, they turned tail and left, deciding uncoupling might be better … less work … and realizing their hearts were not in it. But the Healys had done their homework and were here for the long haul.

"Okay then," Gwen continued. "What is it you do, Mr. Healy?"

"I'm an accountant for the power company, PSE&G," he answered.

"Ah," she said, unsurprised. "And you, Mrs. Healy?"

"I freelance write when I can," she said. "But for the past twelve years, I've been a stay-at-home mom. I do have an opportunity to enter the workforce if need be. I used to work for *Newsday* before the children. They have a co-op position available if I choose."

That was good to hear. A judge could not claim her clients were trying to stay together because one of them didn't want to work. "Well, that's good. You have two children, correct?"

Sara nodded. "Avery is fourteen and Sam is eleven. I may be a stay-at-home mom, but we've always divided our childrearing duties, and that won't change."

Gwen rolled her chair up to the desk, suppressing the snort of laughter that threatened to rise from her throat. "That's good to hear. The judge will expect proof that parenting will not be one-sided."

She wished she did not have to feel so bitter about these things. But getting espoused was a nasty, nasty business. How could she not become jaded?

"We'll need to file a motion with a reason for the espouse. Have you thought about that? Such as, you don't want your children to have stepparents? Or maybe you are not interested in having another partner? Or the reason used most often, you are still very much in love?"

"Well," began Tom hesitantly, "since New York is now a no-fault espouse state, we'd like to use irreconcilable concurrence." Tom traced his fingers over Sara's massive diamond solitaire wedding ring. Sara looked at him and batted her eyelashes.

"Okay," said Gwen, smiling. "You two have done your homework! We will say irreconcilable concurrence, stating parties are 'still in love.'"

"Do you think the judge will force a six-month separation? We know this was standard for years, but a couple of our friends who espoused weren't forced to do it," said Sara, with worry in her voice.

Gwen did not look up but continued to write notes. "Probably not. Judges usually don't want to add any additional strain to an already stressful process. Although, they will still insist on uncoupling counseling. That has not changed!"

"We haven't told the kids yet," Tom said, a little embarrassed.

"Well, we just wanted to wait until after we spoke with you," Sara hurriedly chimed in. "We have notified the school and spoken to the guidance counselor who suggested the school's in-house espouse group counseling sessions. They feel it's good for the kids to know they are not alone in this situation."

Gwen put down her pen and looked up at the two of them. "It seems to me you've put in a lot of time, thought, and research about espousing. You took the right steps for your children, which will reflect well in front of a judge."

Sara let out a huge sigh and looked over at Tom. "Well, I guess we should get started on all the paperwork!"

Gwen put her notepad to the side, picked up a manila folder with the word "Healy" printed on it, and opened it to show a large stack of documents. "Okay, let's begin. We start with the complaint and summons we need to file with the court, which is the petition for dissolution of uncoupling. Then in a few weeks, we will receive a summons date to appear before the court, and we'll ask the judge for leniency on uncoupling rules."

This was where Gwen usually lost a portion of her potential clients. But the Healys had proven they were prepared as Gwen watched Sara pull out two pens from her purse—one for her and presumably one for Tom.

"And then, of course, comes the trial. We will compile all the evidence to bolster the claim you two should stay together. If the judge agrees to your motion, he or she will write up a decree of espouse, and finally, you two will be together forever."

Tom slid to the edge of his seat and grabbed one of the pens from Sara's hand, ready and willing to sign his life away. He grinned at Gwen. "Let's do this."

Gwen nodded and pulled out the first set of papers. She looked over at them mournfully, thinking again, *Oh boy, a couple of lovesick puppies.*

"All right. Let's get started."

CHAPTER 2

The Judge

CARLY ABRAHAM PEERED DOWN through her bifocals from her bench at the Suffolk County Third District Court, looking at the couple in front of her.

Kadir Passud, Judge Abraham's assistant, handed her the petitioner's motion. Kadir had been Judge Abraham's assistant since he was fresh out of Hofstra Law School. His chocolate brown eyes, russet-brown skin, and seductive smile could make any girl fall in love. But for the most part, he was serious as a heart attack and did his job well. Kadir had a pretty wife and daughter, married for some years and probably near uncoupling. Or so Abraham thought. She tried not to get too close to anyone.

Shaking her head, she glanced at the motion in front of her. The Martins, Ann and Joseph; married fourteen years and due to uncouple in the next eight months. Every once in a while, Judge Abraham came across a star-crossed, lovestruck couple who refused to let the outside world intrude on their little lovefest, believing they were made for each other for life.

Enough to make any sane person lose her lunch.

Ann and Joseph? They weren't that kind of couple, thank God for small favors. But still, uncoupling was a law for a reason. People who went against it annoyed the hell out of the judge. All it meant was more work for her, more people to clog her courtroom. Why couldn't people just fall in line and uncouple? Uncoupling worked for millions of people. Uncoupling had worked for her. It was the natural order of things. It made sense.

The motion stated that the Josephs were filing against the uncoupling because of "irreconcilable concurrence." Everyone was using that one nowadays. Easy out! But reading further, the desire to espouse typically came down to the fact that they couldn't decide on child custody, or who would take the "other" house and have to move, as well as a couple of other sticking points. Whatever it was, they felt it was easier to just remain married.

Some people were simply born to go against the grain and create trouble.

Judge Abraham, at least, could handle these.

It was the other kind, the goofily happy, pathetically in-tune, "finish each other's sentences" type that she hated.

She'd seen too many of them in her career. It was wholly disgusting how in love some people could be. Didn't anyone ever think of the kids?

No wonder she was bitter. It was that side of humanity that sometimes made her think there was no real justice on earth and that her career as a district judge was nothing but a sham.

Robert Feinstein, the prosecutor who represented the State of New York against those who wanted to espouse, hung on the bench and whispered, "Same shit, different day, huh?"

Judge Abraham sighed and grimaced at Feinstein. Graying, tall, with a distinguished and unforgettable face, he was maybe her age, a little older, and getting closer to the end of his career. He might be the only person who was as jaded as she was when it came to hearing these cases. He, like her, had been uncoupled after his first marriage and never sought marriage again. At least he was sensible that way. "Once was enough, eh Carly," Feinstein had once quipped. "That's Judge Abraham to you," she'd replied. Just because they worked together was no reason to get that familiar. She'd earned the right to be called Judge, and she wasn't going to let a smarmy, golden-tongued prosecutor charm his way into her heart.

That was the problem with Feinstein. He was entirely too cavalier, too easygoing. People trying to espouse was no laughing matter. The judge didn't always like the way he behaved in her court.

Judge Abraham waved Feinstein back to his table and motioned her assistant, Kadir, to the bench.

"What's your take on these two?" she whispered to Kadir while eyeing the couple.

"These two" weren't in love, thank God. That always did a number on Judge Abraham's stomach. Graphic PDAs from people who shouldn't even be together anymore were simply gross.

"Not too smart. Lazy. The uncouple counselor, Dr. Reed, stated in her report that she didn't see any reason for not uncoupling. I don't think they are particularly in love. They just believe it's easier to stay together," replied Kadir matter-of-factly.

She nodded and motioned Kadir away from the bench. That was

her take as well. Sometimes adults acted like children, doing what was best for themselves rather than what was good for everyone involved.

"Mr. Martin," she said, addressing the husband as he poured himself a glass of water. He was bursting out of his suit like a sausage in a casing, with his tie askew. He pulled on it uncomfortably. "It says here that you can't agree on custody. Were the children consulted?"

"Child, Your Honor," Mr. Martin said, clearing his throat. He looked at his wife, who frowned at him. "No. She's—she's only three. She doesn't really understand what is going on, but I feel, um, I mean, we feel she would be upset if we changed our living situation."

That was always a problem. The longer a couple waited to produce children, the greater the possibility of objecting when it came time to uncouple.

"Well. Little children always want both parents on hand, but when they are older, they understand how normal uncoupling is," she said, for what seemed like the thousandth time in her career.

Mrs. Martin's brow knitted with worry. "Yes, but ..."

"No. Look," Judge Abraham boomed, loud enough that everyone in the courtroom stopped what they were doing and took notice. "If I took every three-year-old's concerns seriously, I'd likely end up granting espouse decrees to everyone. But uncoupling exists for a reason. On top of that, Dr. Reed wrote—" Judge Abraham put on her glasses to read from a document on her desk—"'There was no reason for the uncoupling not to move forward; no evidence of attachment between the couple, the child too young for any opinion, and no evidence of the financial need for codependence.'"

Judge Abraham looked up from the document and said, "Suck it up and be parents to your child. Do the right and normal thing here! Believe me, you'll thank me for this lesson when he's a teenager."

Mrs. Martin, berated, hung her head. Mr. Martin opened his mouth to say something, his lips forming the beginnings of several challenges, but then he stopped and looked over to his lawyer for some help. Before the lawyer could say anything, though …

"You have issues with the regular uncoupling custody guidelines?" the judge asked.

The Custody Guidelines were given to all couples when they obtained a marriage license. They urged those soon to be wed to plan for the future, which included the family they wanted in fifteen years, since at that time, uncoupling custody issues would come into play. In the case of just one child, the usual uncoupling custody scenario was either one parent got weekends, the other, weekdays, or they took one week on and one week off. It worked well.

"Well," Mr. Martin began. He seemed afraid to speak, which Judge Abraham relished. She loved being the judge whom people feared. "Yes. We can't seem to decide who will get Violet on weekends and who will get her during the week. We both work full time, you see. Long hours."

Judge Abraham rolled her eyes and looked down at the documents in front of her. "It says here that Violet is in day care? And you can modify the schedule so you each get one day on the weekend, and a few days during the week, if you find that to be fairer. You can work out the details with Mr. Feinstein."

The couple looked at each other, frowning.

"What I really have a hard time understanding," the judge went on, "is how the two of you can think that espouse is the answer to this. The child doesn't currently dictate the parenting schedule in your family, does he?"

The two looked at her blankly.

Kadir looked up from his notes and raised a finger.

"What is it, Kadir?" she grumbled.

"It's a she," he said, pointing to the motion. "Violet."

"Whatever," the judge mumbled, clearing her throat importantly. "We are the adults. We are the ones who make the decisions for the best of our families. Not our kids. If we let children determine the rules, I'm sure we'd all be eating Froot Loops every day of the week. This is totally ridiculous."

Her voice had been steadily rising. Now, it echoed off every wall in the courtroom. Every face in the gallery was staring at her. *Good.* That would show them not to mess with her. She liked that.

The judge could have given their lawyer more trouble; after all, discovery hadn't gone smoothly, the required documents had been hastily assembled, and the timeline entirely unsatisfactory, but their lawyer was a little blonde fresh out of law school. Shayna ... something. She looked to be about two seconds from running from the courtroom in tears, never to return. Judge Abraham was going to end this charade.

"You've been brought here to prove your case for espousing, but to me, all you've proven is that you're both ill-prepared and do not really know what you want, or what's good for your family. So, I suppose I need to make this decision."

The woman's face was bright red. The man stammered to reply but only uttered, "Ur ..."

The judge waited patiently, but she was not known for her patience. One beat, two. Time's up.

She slammed the gavel down and said, "Espouse denied. This case is adjourned. Next."

The judge had a full docket of cases to hear this morning, and she wanted to be free to play tennis with the ladies at the club. She was the only one of them who was not yet retired because, unlike many of them, she liked her job.

She enjoyed arguing with people. She loved being right, especially about uncoupling.

Judge Abraham looked over at Kadir as the Martin couple filed out, heads down, thoroughly humiliated. "Wow, Judge," Kadir said with a spry smirk on his face. "Way to strip them of all their dignity."

"Well, you know what happens if they leave with their dignity intact," she grumbled, thrusting the file aside as he passed her the papers for the next case. "They may decide to file an appeal."

Judge Abraham looked at the next file, a sticky note with the message, "Don't be too hard on these folks; remember to save some energy for tennis." Kadir and his kind heart. She pulled off the sticky note and tossed it over her shoulder. Still, Kadir was a rule-follower, and Judge Abraham knew he was a believer in the uncoupling laws.

She opened the next file. More of the same. Judge Abraham gave a little sneer. *Bring it!*

CHAPTER 3

The Kids

SAM HEALY SAT OUTSIDE Oldfield Middle School, nose pressed against his cell phone, on a particularly blustery autumn day with fast-moving black clouds that looked about as angry as he felt.

He was not one of those kids who constantly fiddled on his phone, getting text-neck and walking into fountains or bushes. He was a smart, studious kid who got As in everything. But today, as he scrolled through a bunch of Snaps from his friends—friends who all looked so darn happy and carefree—he wanted nothing more than for his phone to swallow him up.

His older sister, Avery, nudged him. "Be careful; Dad's going to flip if you use up all his data."

"Who are you kidding?" he muttered. "There are four people in the family, and you use most of it."

They were sitting on the corner waiting for their parents to pick them up after another stellar Monday. He had forgotten his trumpet for band practice and had to use one of the "school instruments" that was badly out of tune and whose mouthpiece smelled like Cool Ranch Doritos. He'd tripped in flag football and gotten a face full of dirt plus two bloody knees. And then ... then there were his parents. Why were Mondays even invented? It seemed like that was the day everything went wrong.

But yeah, he did not need any problems with his dad. He pulled his head out of the phone and scanned Greenlawn Road to see if his dad's blue Range Rover was on its way. Nope.

Avery had her earbuds in, probably listening to some lame boy band. He envied the way she never let anything bother her. She was just too cool, except around James the Perfect; James Baum, whom she'd had a crush on since she was nine. Sam guessed that if he wanted to make her show some emotion, all he would have to do was record his sister's phone conversations with her best friend, Scarlet. *Oh, James is so hot! And he's just so awesome!*

Just then, a couple of hands dropped over his glasses, blinding him from the outside world. They smelled like gummy worms. Cara Baum, James's freakishly annoying younger sister, was always eating gummies, worms and bears and fish; it was surprising she still had teeth. "Guess who!" she chortled.

Sam groaned and wrenched her hands away from his face. "Cut it out, lame wad."

Cara grinned and pranced around to the front of the bench, motioning him to move over so she could sit beside him. Fat chance. He was not moving.

Avery suddenly stood up, bit her lip, and did this weird, hip-jutting-out pose that she thought was cool but really made her look like a flamingo on one leg. A second later, James appeared, wearing sunglasses despite all signs that the sky was about to pour rain. He had his hands in his pockets and was slouching with his backpack slung over one shoulder. "What up?" he said to Sam, his voice impossibly deep and masculine. *When had* that *happened?*

"Hey," Sam replied, his voice still squeaky like a little kid.

Anaya Passud was standing nearby with her nose in a book. Anaya, the quiet, studious one, was even more hardcore about schoolwork than Sam was. Sam was not sure how Anaya put up with Avery. About a billion years ago, the two of them had made sense as best friends, but now Anaya was a straight-A student, leader of the math bowl, and president of the student council. Avery was a solid C student and often lamented that if things like curling iron usage were taught in school, she'd get straight As. That, and she could not seem to concentrate on anything other than boys.

Well, not all boys. Mainly just James.

Most of the girls at Oldfield had a thing for James. He and his best friend, Rob, were number one on the popularity charts. Unlike Sam. Sam was round and wore glasses and had his small, tight group of friends. But he wasn't in the same popular circle as Avery and James. Sometimes he wished that life could go back to when it was easy, and the five of them used to hang out in each other's backyards, playing pirates or highway patrol or whatever.

"So," Cara said, sitting down in the space vacated by Avery and jostling Sam's shoulder. "Why were you so quiet today?"

Sam shrugged as he always did around Cara these days.

Cara had been his best friend for forever. But lately, things had changed. Now, everything she said and did annoyed the crap out of him. He told her not to hang on him or touch him, to just be cool, but that didn't stop her. His buddies were always ragging on him, asking how she kissed, as if they were a real couple. Gross.

"Turn that frown upside down!" She spit out the words like a cheerleader and did arm movements to match. She *was* a cheerleader, like Avery, but junior varsity. He wouldn't admit how good she looked in those skirts. He hated himself for noticing.

His frown deepened at the thought.

She grabbed his arm and jiggled it. "It can't be that bad!"

"Yeah it is," he muttered. "I think my parents are going to espouse."

Cara's jaw dropped. "What?"

Avery kicked at him. "Shut up, doofus," she muttered. "God, you're so lame."

Cara covered her mouth with her hands as if she'd just witnessed the most horrific car accident.

"Are you kidding me? That's horrible. That means you won't get two Christmases. Two vacations. Two birthdays. Two homes ... Oh, God. Why are they doing that?"

James pulled his sister's glossy dark ponytail. "Hey. Cool it." He turned to Avery, who was looking at her brother with a combination of shock and embarrassment. "I'm sorry. That sucks."

"'S okay, no big deal. We don't really know ... I mean, my parents haven't said anything to us yet. We just heard them talking one night … you know parents ... they think their kids are stupid," Avery said with a shrug. Then she beamed up at him. "But thanks. How are things with your parents?"

He shrugged. "Awesome. They love being uncoupled. Like, they're both alive again. Seriously, they should have done it years ago."

Sam sighed wistfully at the thought of that. That normalcy. That was the way things were supposed to go. Why did their parents have to be such freaks?

James looked at Anaya, who stood off to the side, paging through, of all things, a dictionary, and quietly biting her lip. Anaya would never be caught scrolling through her iPhone; as far as Sam knew, she didn't even have a phone. "What about your parents? Their uncoupling is coming up, isn't it?" James asked.

She stopped with her finger on a word, her mouth moving silently over the pronunciation. "What? Oh. Yeah. In a few months."

They waited for her to volunteer more, but she didn't. She went right back to her dictionary.

Sam thought Anaya was being strangely quiet about the whole uncoupling thing. He would have liked the discussion to change to where Anaya's second home was going to be located, her new visiting arrangements, and all the other things kids discussed when their parents, normal parents, uncoupled.

Uncoupling was an awesome rite of passage, like winning the kids' lottery.

The fact was that most of their parents were heading for that crucial uncoupling date. That's the way it worked in middle school. While a good majority of the parents quietly uncoupled while their kids were this age, occasionally, maybe once or twice in each class, you'd hear of one family that decided to initiate espouse proceedings. The poor kids of those parents would undoubtedly become the butt of the schoolyard jokes and mean gossip. It was worse than an embarrassing Instagram or everyone finding out about your crush.

Sam really wished it didn't have to be him. As it was, growing up was hard enough. Avery was popular; she'd survive it. But Sam? Sam was teetering on the edge of obscurity. One wrong move would seal his loser status in permanent marker.

"Just keep your mouth shut about it, okay?" he grumbled at Cara.

"I'm sorry, Sammy," she whispered.

Sammy. Cara was the only one who called him that, leftover from the days they used to play together after school. He hated how much he liked that nickname. She was so close to him now, smelling of gummy bears and bubble gum lip gloss. He refused to look at her. That would probably make him go all googly-eyed. Instead, he gave her one of his *Whatever* shrugs.

He was still sulking when Mrs. Baum came to pick up Cara and James. She was a sensible woman. Fashionable. She was wearing jeans, a button-down white shirt, knee-height brown boots, and a well-worn jean jacket. Happily uncoupled, as she was supposed to be, and now living it up during her second chance at singledom.

But Sam's parents?

Freaks. They were so in love that they'd both let themselves go. They were probably so lost in love with their freaky espouse idea that they'd forgotten what time it was, namely time for Sam and Avery to be picked up from school.

Sam rolled his eyes in disgust and jabbed in a text to his mother. Lame, lame, lame.

CHAPTER 4

Gwen's First Love

SARA HEALY WIGGLED the fingers of her right hand, cracked her knuckles, and smiled at Gwen. "You weren't kidding when you said there was a lot of paperwork. I feel like I just wrote a novel, longhand."

Thomas signed the bottom of the last form and capped his pen. "Signed, sealed, delivered."

"I'm yours," they said in unison, giving each other silly grins.

Not even close, Gwen thought. *Unfortunately, we're just at the starting line of this race.*

"Oh, dear," Sara said. She looked up from her phone and frowned at her husband. "It's after four. Sam just texted us from the school."

Thomas shot up, flustered. He looked at his phone. No text. "I didn't get a text?" he said, seemingly annoyed.

Gwen kept her head down while gathering up all the documents to put into the folder and thought, *They will have to make sure the kids understand that moving forward, both parents should be on the text string. Sara is not going to be the exclusive parent picking them up in the future. Even though we're filing espouse papers, there's no saying a judge will grant them one if they can't show it is not all about convenience for the parents. I'll cover that in our next meeting.*

Thomas pocketed his phone and said, "Are we done here? I'm sorry, but we didn't realize the time … you see, we have to pick up the kids."

"I understand!" Gwen said, standing and squeezing around her desk. She walked the happy couple to the door. They were already holding hands despite all the trauma those hands had gone through during the marathon signing session. Gwen wasn't sure she'd ever seen any grown adults so completely … lovesick. "You two enjoy your evening. I'll file the paperwork tomorrow and let you know when the hearing is set for."

Once again, the two were gazing so intently at each other that Gwen had the distinct feeling of intruding upon them, even though they were in the foyer of her own home.

She watched them until the trance was broken and they finally noticed that she was still standing there. "Oh. Yes, thank you," Sara said, shaking her hand.

Thomas nodded at Gwen, and she shook his hand as well. "Thank you again for putting your trust in me."

Closing the heavy door, Gwen leaned against it and sighed. Sometimes she felt like no matter what she did to explain what a couple was in for, they just didn't get it. The Healys were clearly in a love bubble. They wouldn't understand until they went through it. This was war. A bloody, exhausting, all-consuming battle. But if they truly loved each other, an espouse decree would be granted, and they would live happily ever after … hopefully!

Gwen flattened her hair into her bun and wiped at her shiny nose. She still liked putting care into her appearance around Dennis. Although, no matter how bad she looked these days, he always said she looked beautiful. Force of habit; after twenty-six years of marriage, she had no intention of stopping now.

As she crossed the lacquered floor of the foyer, she heard Riya in Dennis's room, humming "Sweet Caroline" as she worked. When Gwen peeked inside, Riya was just setting up a tray for Dennis's dinner.

"Hello, Mrs. Stevens," Riya said with a smile. Riya, who was short and small-boned with beautiful red-brown skin and long dark brown hair tied back in a ponytail, adjusted the utensils on the tray for Dennis.

Gwen had never seen the woman in anything other than hospital scrubs, yet Riya always seemed to glow in her beauty. "Was that the Healys I just saw leaving?"

Gwen nodded. "You know them?"

"Yes. Their daughter Avery and my Anaya used to be practically joined at the hip," she said, her face dissolving into a frown. "Not so much now. Tween years drama. Girl drama."

Gwen nodded, though she couldn't begin to understand. Her girl-hood days were long past, and she and Dennis's parenting expertise only contained boy drama. Terrell was twenty-five now and was sedate, like his father. He wasn't the type for theatrics. He was remarkably level-headed, despite never having had parents who uncoupled, like most of his friends' parents. Gwen was Dennis's second marriage, and second marriages were immune from uncoupling laws. Gwen had always been worried that Terrell had missed out, not having parents who uncoupled, but Terrell didn't seem to mind. Gwen and Dennis had sent Terrell to therapy just in case he was having issues with them not uncoupling, but he refused to go to any more sessions after the first.

Gwen sat on the edge of her husband's bed, wishing there was a pillow to fluff or a glass of water to hold to his lips or something she could do to make herself feel useful. But no, Riya was too good and efficient for that. Gwen settled for patting his hand. "How's the patient?"

Before Riya could answer, Dennis grumbled, "The patient is right here and not on his last breath. He can still answer perfectly well on his own."

Riya said, "She asks me because I'm the expert. Whenever she asks you, you always answer the same. *I'm fine.*"

Gwen nodded in agreement. "Right as rain," she said, mimicking his jovial inflection. Dennis was usually jovial. The grumbling was a recent development, added to his personality with the colon cancer diagnosis six months earlier. Though cancer had given Dennis the grumbles, it had stripped other things from him: his pink-cheeked color, the extra pounds that Gwen used to like to cuddle at night, and most of his energy. "I don't think rain is very right. I like sunshine."

Dennis waved her away. "You two don't have to fuss over me like mother hens."

"I'm your wife, and she's your nurse," Gwen said, shaking her head. "It's our job!"

Riya pushed the food tray on wheels closer to Dennis's bedside. Her voice was sober, calming. "He is having a good day, Gwen. His vitals are good, lots of energy, and he had a healthy BM."

Dennis rubbed his grizzled jowls and gave Riya an annoyed look over his bifocals that said, *Really?* Poor Dennis. Once one of the most respected espouse attorneys in the state of New York, he had lately been reduced to something akin to a toddler. Adults spoke about him, not to him, and they discussed things like his bodily functions with great excitement. For a man who'd once been so vital, so fierce, Gwen knew this had to be frustrating.

But as hard as it was for him, it wasn't exactly easy on Gwen. The first time she had seen Dennis, nearly thirty years ago, he'd been presenting an espouse case in front of a packed courtroom. He'd looked so damn good in that suit, so confident, so immortal. She'd been in love with him from that very moment.

And now?

Now, the love was still there and just as intense, but everything else was so different.

Fighting back tears, she looked at his tray. "Grilled cheese and applesauce. Your favorite," she said to him, but only when the words were out did she realize how much she sounded like a mother talking to a preschool-aged Terrell.

It didn't go unnoticed. Dennis's body might have been failing him, but his mind was still as sharp as ever. "I never was fond of grilled cheese," he muttered, giving her a sour look.

"I can get you something else?" Riya put in.

Dennis just shook his head. He loved grilled cheese, and Gwen knew it.

Dennis picked up the crust and started to nibble at his sandwich as Riya said again, "So the Healys are getting espoused?"

Gwen nodded, "Keep it under your hat, okay?" Riya smiled and nodded. In Gwen's experience, Riya's switch was usually stuck on happy, but Gwen could see the question in Riya's eyes. After all, Riya and her husband, Kadir, would be reaching their uncoupling date in the next year or so. Riya had indicated to Gwen that she wanted to bring up the espouse option, but Kadir was always busy working, and she hadn't broached the subject.

"Have you seen Kadir at all at the courthouse?" Riya asked in a casual tone.

Yes, Gwen had, numerous times, almost once a week. But Riya knew that. Gwen felt she was fishing for something.

"Yes, but ..." Gwen answered, quizzically, "we haven't really spoken except for a 'good morning' or 'good afternoon.'"

"Oh, sure." A flash of disappointment clouded Riya's dark eyes, and a tiny wrinkle of three lines appeared on the bridge of her nose. It was a blink-and-you-miss-it thing, though, as Riya's bad moods always were. "Of course."

"He's obviously busy, Riya," Gwen assured her. "You know, working for that witch of a judge is probably like running on a hamster wheel—"

"I'm assuming you're talking about Carly," Dennis said.

Gwen stopped short. In her ongoing struggle to stop treating her husband like a toddler, she'd gone and once again forgotten he was in the room, casually chewing on his dinner and listening to their every word. He'd called her Carly, not Judge Abraham or The Wicked Witch of the Bench, which was what she was better known as downtown. Well, what else would he call her after being married to her for fifteen years? But still. It was enough to get every hair on her neck and arms standing at attention.

Her cheeks burned, and her nostrils flared. "Don't go sticking up for that woman," Gwen snapped. "You know she's a nasty, cold-hearted, wicked bi—"

She stopped suddenly when her husband lurched forward, his twig-like body wracked with a convulsive coughing fit.

Gwen and Riya rushed forward to help settle him down. "I'm sorry. I'm sorry," Gwen repeated over and over again. She lifted water to his lips for him to drink, and eventually, he caught his breath again.

"I don't think I'm hungry anymore," he said quietly, pushing the plate away. "I think I'll rest."

That was par for the course. He'd shed so much weight that he was merely a shadow of the man she'd known. Gwen wished he would eat as much as he rested.

Riya cleaned up his meal and walked out to the kitchen with Gwen following, shutting the door behind her.

"So?" Gwen said as Riya scraped the remains of Dennis's food into the trash can. "Do you think he's getting better?"

Riya shrugged. "Well, I can't tell for sure. Except for this coughing fit, it was a very good day. When is his next PET scan?"

"Next week," Gwen said with a nervous sigh. "I just wish we didn't have to wait. I really could use some good news right now and so could he. He has the spirit, Riya, and he's a tough son of a gun. If anyone can fight this and win, it's him. But there are only so many setbacks a person can face before being beaten down. This chemo trial better work. It just has to."

Gwen's shoulders slumped, and Riya put a hand on Gwen's forearm. "It will. It did. He seems stronger today. Really."

Gwen smiled at her, hoping and praying that Riya wasn't telling her a lie. Her husband, the love of her life, the man she'd devoted twenty-six years on this earth to, good and bad, might be dying.

No, she refused to admit to that right now. Gwen had to think positive thoughts. For Dennis and for her sanity.

CHAPTER 5

That Did Not Go Well

"WOW, DAD, 5:30?" Avery asked as they trudged into their modest seventies-style split-level house in Greenlawn. "So *expedient*."

Sara Healy let out a sigh, wishing Tom hadn't bought her that SAT vocabulary book for her thirteenth birthday. Avery wouldn't ever let him live that down. *Other kids are getting new phones for their entry into teen-hood, and I get a freaking book?* she'd complained. While getting any special treatment for entering one's teen years seemed silly to Sara, the vocab book seemed sillier yet. Avery wasn't the studying type, and the SAT tests were still nearly four years away. But Avery had managed to memorize several words to use out of spite whenever she really wanted to annoy her loving, anxious parents.

The kids piled their too-heavy backpacks into the mudroom along with their sneakers and jackets. Avery's phone dinged with a text for the thirtieth time in the twelve minutes since they'd picked the kids up at Oldfield Middle School. She surreptitiously checked it before rushing off to her bedroom.

"Homework first!" Sara called after her, looking over at Sam, who had taken out his social studies textbook. *Good boy.* At least she'd gotten it 50 percent right when it came to parenting. At this point, that was the best she could hope for.

Sara flipped the lights on in the darkened kitchen and stared at the cold stovetop, wishing dinner would just make itself. When that didn't happen, she opened the refrigerator and dug out some ground beef for tacos.

"Oh, tacos, what a surprise," Tom said with a grin, giving her side a squeeze as he passed her.

She grinned back at him and wondered if the espouse meeting had put any doubts in his mind. He'd been so resolute about espousing, so willing to do absolutely anything to stay together. In fact, Tom was the one who'd first brought up the subject a few years before the uncoupling date. He'd sat Sara down, told her he still loved her madly, and even gave her a rose. It was all so romantic. An espouse proposal. There were plenty of them to view on YouTube. People went to extremes for their espouse proposals—on mountaintops, at halftime during football games, during a romantic picnic in the park. Tom's was heartfelt and simple. Perfect.

Sara was relieved when he'd proposed it because she had been thinking the very same thing. She enjoyed being home with the kids and wasn't sure she wanted to be back in the workforce. Sara adored her life as it was.

But after the meeting with Gwen, she wondered if things would shift between Tom and her. There were lots of obstacles to the espouse process. Did she notice a shift in Tom? Probably all in her imagination.

Yes, it was going to be a lot of work, but Sara and Tom were committed. It would be worth it, no matter what others said. Tom was probably worried about telling the kids.

Sara looked at Sam, busily scribbling on a wide-ruled notebook at the kitchen table. This would be hard on him. He'd been that way, even in the womb—the weather, a too-itchy tag on his T-shirt, the taste of spicy foods—things just affected him deeply. She could put up with all the negatives of the espouse proceedings, but hurting Sam, her poor, sensitive, thoughtful boy, was the one that would sting the most.

That was probably why, out of all the foods in the fridge, Sara had gravitated to the tacos. They were Sam's favorite. Maybe they would help the news go down easier.

Tom set out the plates as Sara chopped the lettuce and tomatoes and browned the meat. That was one thing about the two of them; life was much easier and more comfortable than she could ever imagine it being if they were apart. There was a division of responsibilities. They worked together like a well-oiled machine. Marriage didn't even seem like work to Sara; it just felt natural.

Uncoupling after fifteen years together? *That* felt unnatural.

Maybe, in time, after they got over their shock, the rest of her family and friends would come to understand. At least, she hoped.

Dinner was typical, though Sam seemed uncharacteristically quiet, and Avery tried to sneak her cell phone to the table, texting in her lap until Tom confiscated it. The news of the day was shared: Sara had gotten an assignment for *Newsday* and Tom had gotten the thumbs-up for his work on a big project from senior management. One of Sam's essays was selected as a finalist for the Veteran's Day contest, and Avery just shrugged as if she'd rather be eating with a pack of rabid wolves and said nothing.

Meanwhile, Tom and Sara exchanged looks, each daring the other to bring up the news.

It wasn't until dessert, when they were all sharing some Edy's Rocky Road, that Tom cleared his throat.

Here it is, Sara thought, bracing herself, knowing what was coming.

"We have other news," Tom announced, looking around the table at each of them in turn.

Sam and Avery exchanged a worried glance and then looked at him expectantly.

Have they already guessed? Sara wondered. After all, she had to think that since most of the kids' parents were uncoupling, it had to be a big part of everyday conversation—whose parents were doing it, when, and what the transition to a two-household arrangement would be. Sam was perceptive, so he could have known, but Avery was more wrapped up in herself and the lives of YouTube stars. In fact, Avery had distanced herself so much from Sara and Tom lately that Sara was surprised Avery even looked up whenever she called her daughter's name.

"You know that our uncoupling date is coming up," Sara said as Tom squeezed her hand under the table. "Well ..."

She looked up at Tom, who picked up seamlessly as if they'd rehearsed it. "Even though we have everything set to uncouple—the second house, all the documents are filed, and the parenting schedules ... we thought ... or rather ... we decided, to ..."

Sara smiled, and they both erupted with, "Why do it at all?"

Avery's blank face crumpled. Sam got that worry crinkle in his forehead that showed up whenever he was either thinking too hard or disappointed.

"Please tell me you're doing it. Please. Please. Please," Avery looked at them, clasped her hands together, and let out one last, strangled, "*Please.*"

They didn't answer. For a moment, Sara wondered if it wasn't too late to table this discussion for another time.

"You're getting espoused?" Sam cried, so wounded that his fragile voice cracked. "Really?"

Sara looked at Tom, and they nodded.

"So, you're really going to go through with this?" Avery said, rolling her eyes. "Well, that's just perfect. *Sublime.*"

Another SAT word.

"Hey, guys, it's not like it's the end of the world! We get to stay together in one house, no shuffling between homes, and continue to live the way we are now," Tom announced, trying to jostle Sam's sandy brown hair.

Sam dipped his head away from his well-meaning dad and licked his spoon. He had a chocolate mustache. Sam was the world's messiest eater. "For you maybe," he grumbled.

"Yeah!" Avery piped up, the two of them on the same side for the first time ever. "You don't have to go to a school where you'll end up being the laughingstock of the entire student body."

Tom tried again. "Oh, come on ..."

"I might as well hide my head in a paper bag," Sam sighed.

"That's not enough. I need to suffocate myself with a plastic bag," Avery said dramatically, throwing her spoon down on the table. Chocolate droplets went everywhere. "I might as well go to school in a Walmart wardrobe. Everyone's going to be laughing and talking about me."

"If they laugh at you, just laugh right on back," said their dad.

Sam glared at him. "That only works in your dream world, Dad. In our world, if you do that, you're likely to get your butt kicked."

Avery nodded. "Really, Dad? You have been married to Mom for almost fifteen years! What can possibly be so attractive between the two of you now?"

"Avery!" Sara said, shocked, her skin pinking. She might have been nearing forty, and yes, she had gained some weight and no longer wore the latest styles, but she still considered herself rather attractive. Not a model, but certainly not hideous. "How could you say such a thing about your dad and me?"

Avery gave her a look that said, *Believe me, I know what being attracted to someone looks like.* Sara didn't doubt it. With the way she had caught her daughter looking at the Baum boy, she knew it was only a matter of time before she had to deal with boys and birth control. It was enough to make her want to bury her head in sand, ostrich-style.

Sara suppressed a shudder as Tom said, "It's a good thing that we care about each other, guys. Isn't it?"

"Yeah. Great. But you don't have to live together," Avery snapped. "People who still care about each other uncouple all the time. They don't go ahead and get espoused. That's so lame."

Sam crossed his arms and grimaced at them across the table. "Double lame."

"Triple lame with a cherry on top. Like the lamest thing ever in the history of the world." Avery covered her face with her hands and shook her head. "Can I have my phone back?"

Sara sighed. Gone was any chance of connecting with her daughter as a family, of forging a new bond based on this decision to espouse. Guiltily, Tom wrestled the iPhone out of his pants pocket and placed it on the table. Avery scooped it up and rushed away, probably to text all her friends about her life coming to an end.

Tom stood up and wandered to the trash to wrangle it outside to the garbage can. Sara looked over at Sam for some indication, however tiny, that she had not scarred him permanently.

"Mom," he said softly, timidly, and she could almost see the six-year-old cuddle monster who used to crawl into her bed at night. He was such a little lovebug.

"It's okay," she said soothingly. "You know, no matter what, we'll always love you."

"It's weird, is what it is," he mumbled, his shoulders slumped. "The kids at school all say it's about selfish parents."

"No. No, not true. Yes, it isn't normal. But why shouldn't people do what makes them happy? This—being together—this is what will make your mom and dad happy."

"Eating a whole carton of Oreos makes me happy. But you don't let me do it."

Sara smiled. He was always twisting things around in his head, testing new theories. That was the way his brilliant little mind worked. She said, "Because eventually, that would make you sick. And it's my job to protect you. I don't want to do anything that would hurt you."

Sam nodded, and for the first time, she hoped he was beginning to understand. "But why? Did Avery and I do something? Is it our fault you still want to stay together?"

Oh, my sweet little boy. Always so worried about hurting others. Sara's heart went out to him.

"No, of course not. You're perfect. We just ... we love you and we love us as a family. And your father and I still love each other ... very much. We want to stay together. Keep things the way they are," she said in her baby voice, reaching her hand out to him. "Come on, my little man."

His frown deepened into a scowl, and he pushed away from the table. "I'm not little, and I'm not your man," he muttered. Then he grabbed his textbook and notebook and rushed up the stairs. A second later, the bedroom door slammed with an ear-shattering crash that made the whole house shake.

"Well, that went well," Tom said when he returned, digging into his ice cream and taking a monster bite.

Sara burst out with a laugh, which dwindled to abject misery. She had never seen Sam look so completely distraught before. Maybe they *had* scarred them for life?

"We're doing the right thing, right?" Sara asked, peering at Tom with a questioning look in her eyes.

Tom peeked up from his ice cream, "Give it time. It's not like we are the first ones doing this. Espouse is very common now, especially since the laws are more relaxed that make it easier." He reached across the table, took Sara's hand in his, and spoke firmly. "We are going to get through this fine. I love you, we love the kids, and that is all the strength we need. Have some faith." Tom released Sara's hand, stood up, and said, "Wish me luck. Going to check on the kids." He puffed up his chest and turned and swung his arms back and forth like Popeye.

Sara chuckled, looked into her dish of ice cream, and swirled the melted chocolate, marshmallow, and nuts around with the spoon to see if there were any answers buried somewhere in the dish.

CHAPTER 6

Is This Normal?

THE PASSUD CONDOMINIUM sat on a hilltop overlooking a large pond that was connected to the Long Island Sound. The houses surrounding the pond were large homes built in the early 1900s, all with small docks that moored canoes or kayaks. Inside the condominium, Riya yawned as she reached into the cabinet and took down plates for dinner. It was after eight o'clock, but since both Passuds had long work schedules, this was the norm.

Anaya, hearing the dishes clattering, sat up dutifully from her perch in the window seat where she'd been reading *To Kill a Mockingbird*, and hurried to fulfill her dinner chore. She set the kitchen table precisely, a trait from her father, making sure the napkins were folded and the forks were lined up as if they weren't just eating a quick, greasy meal out of paper cartons from the Thai place down the street.

"How was your day, dear?" Riya asked her daughter as the girl scuttled around the kitchen table.

"I got an A on that algebra test," she said.

That was no surprise. What stood out in Anaya's days were usually her grades. Anaya never mentioned anything social. Riya had to wonder if Anaya had any close friends. She certainly never discussed Avery or other girls. Anaya used to bring up how Avery, who used to be her best friend, had snubbed her. It had bothered her, then. But now, either she'd gotten over it, or she just accepted it. Riya supposed there were worse things a girl could be into than her schoolwork. "Fantastic!" she replied.

Kadir came down a moment later, freshly showered and wearing sweatpants with a long-sleeved Nike shirt. He always showered after a long day at work, and Riya suspected it was to get all that nasty business of espouse proceedings off his body.

He gave Riya a kiss and padded in slippered feet to the paper bag, peering inside. "Pad thai, eh? It's like you read my mind," he said with a grin.

Well, if you read my mind, you wouldn't be leaving me hanging like this, she thought as he brought the cartons out and opened them. As always, he filled her plate first, then Anaya's, before taking anything for himself.

They sat down. Riya twirled the noodles around her fork and tried to think of something to say. Some funny anecdotes from her day. She needed something casual and benign as a lead-in to the subject she really wanted to broach.

Nothing came. Probably because she was dealing with a very sick man, and what was funny about that? She never asked Kadir how his day was because he'd told her that he didn't want to think of work while he was home.

Before she could think of something, Kadir said, "Felt like it was going to snow today. Too cold for October."

Riya nodded. Truthfully, she'd barely noticed the weather.

Kadir looked at Anaya. "How was school today?"

"I got an A on that algebra test," she repeated.

"Hey. Good job, kiddo," he said, reaching over and giving her shoulder a massage.

Riya could barely take it anymore. Finally, she took a sip of her wine and said, "The Healys were over at Gwen's today."

He stopped chewing and looked intently at his food. "Oh, yeah? They're espousing?"

She nodded. She wanted to say, *Maybe it's time we decide what we're going to do?* But as much as she wanted to figure it out, to get it out in the open and talk about it, she was afraid of his answer.

Kadir had gone to law school not because he wanted to get rich or because he wanted to have some letters to attach to his name. No, he went because he had a deep appreciation and respect for the country's laws. For all laws. They, he said, were what separated us from animals. Therefore, he followed them to the letter. He often told her that laws were in place for a reason: They made us our best selves, and by going against them, even marginally, the human race might as well dissolve into anarchy.

So, no rolling through stop signs for him. No jaywalking. No fudging on his taxes.

No. Riya was *terrified* of his answer because she knew what it would be. He'd follow the uncoupling laws just as he followed the rest.

Kadir just smirked and said, "Hope they don't get Abraham to hear their case. Lady's on an absolute tear. She eviscerated a couple today."

"Oh?"

"Yeah. Sometimes I think she could make people suicidal."

Riya blanched.

"Speaking of which, did we get the Proof of Uncoupling paperwork in the mail?" he asked, oblivious to her consternation as he shoved a forkful of pad thai into his mouth.

She nodded, standing, and went to retrieve the form on the dining room table, set out with all the other mail she hadn't had time to sort through and take care of. Nobody used formal dining rooms anymore; theirs was both a makeshift office and a homework desk for Anaya.

The Proof of Uncoupling form was submitted annually to the county to show their uncoupling plans, how much was saved for the second house, ensuring they'd kept separate bank accounts, that sort of thing. There were rules one had to follow for uncoupling, and the forms were sent in every year like annual taxes.

"I haven't had a chance to look at it," she said, handing it to him, hoping he'd take notice of the uncoupling date printed at the top of the form. Less than a year away. "I know it needs both of our signatures, so you should take a look, too."

He studied the form, scratching at his smooth jawline. "I can get the info together if you're too busy with Dennis. How's the guy doing, by the way?"

Riya shook her head. "Good days and bad days. It's been a bit of a roller coaster going through this new chemo clinical trial. Gwen is terribly stressed."

Riya looked across the table and realized that Anaya was sitting, her fork frozen halfway between the plate and her mouth, staring at the paper. "Is that ... so, do you mean you guys are going to just uncouple in, like, a few months?"

Kadir stared at Anaya. Riya stared back at him, waiting, breathless, for his answer.

"Well, that's the law, and what most normal people do," he said levelly, glancing only for a beat at Riya.

Anaya had big, dark eyes like her mother's, but she could be gloomy and moody like Kadir. She let out a huff of air. "Well, since when are we normal?"

"What?" Kadir said. "You don't think we're normal?"

"I don't understand. I mean, I know, uncoupling is supposed to be good for us. Aren't things good already, the way they are? Why do they have to change?" Anaya burst out the words, dropping her fork to her plate with a clatter.

Riya eyed Kadir calmly. *Anaya is acting like this is some kind of surprise. This happens to almost everyone.*

She gathered her composure and spoke softly to Anaya. "Of course, we will discuss the parenting schedule with you … when the time arrives. What do you think about that?"

"Does it even matter what I think?" she said flatly.

Kadir and Riya stared at each other. Most kids counted the days until their parents uncoupled because it was like Christmas and their birthdays, all rolled into one. They were excited about it. Anaya looked as if they had scheduled her a date with the executioner.

Kadir said, "Of course, it matters what you think. Although, I don't understand the issue. You are behaving as if uncoupling is not normal? This is life. It's normal. It's a very civil thing to do, Anaya."

Riya stared at him, her blood running cold. So, she was right. Kadir wanted to uncouple. But would it be okay? Riya wasn't sure.

Anaya pushed away from the table, grabbed *To Kill a Mockingbird*, and stormed up the stairs to her bedroom.

Riya wished she could do the same thing. She could barely bring herself to look at Kadir, but she turned and gave him a warm smile. Maybe she should contest the uncoupling. Riya had heard stories of one partner in the marriage contesting the uncoupling to gain more time to convince the other partner to espouse. It rarely ever worked—but it did force the couple to stay together longer. Did she want to force Kadir into something he didn't want to do?

No, she loved him too much.

CHAPTER 7

This Is Not Good

THE TREES SWAYED and the leaves fell on another cold morning that painted frost all over the lawns and windshields. But as cold as it was outside, nothing compared to what it was like inside the Passud household. Kadir practically had icicles growing off the end of his nose.

Riya had given him the cold shoulder the entire evening after dinner the night before. She went to her bedroom to read and was asleep before he even made it upstairs. She hadn't set the alarm for his normal six a.m. wake-up or the timer on the coffee machine for him.

Those two things? It meant trouble with a capital T.

Kadir knew it was because of the uncoupling issue. Could Riya blame him for not wanting to discuss it? Whenever it was brought up, a purple vein bulged on Riya's temple and her voice went up an octave.

Did Riya want to espouse? *Now that's a crazy thought!*

She'd heard the horror stories, though he tried not to discuss the really bad stuff. Riya knew about these poor couples going through espouse and all the ridiculous hoops they had to jump through. Espousing was hell.

Did Riya want to put Anaya through that?

That was another thing. Anaya questioning the uncoupling? Like she wanted them to stay together? Anaya had always marched to the beat of her own drummer, but she couldn't seriously want her parents to espouse! Really? He'd been thirteen once, too, and Kadir remembered all the ribbing received by the kids whose parents espoused. You might as well have had a big red LOSER emblem sewn onto your chest.

Kadir spilled hot coffee on his blazer as he rushed; he would be twenty minutes late for court. He downed it as he pulled out of their driveway, scalding his tongue. When he got to downtown Huntington and rushed up the stairs of the courthouse, he knew he was in deep trouble, and not just with the ladies of his family.

Judge Abraham abhorred lateness. The judge had made her last clerk stand in a corner when he was late! He knew she would rip him apart like a misbehaving child.

Luckily, court wasn't in session until nine. Kadir rushed into the judge's chambers, noticing too late that his tie was askew.

Judge Abraham peered up from her papers and said, "Late again."

Again. She made it seem like he did it all the time. In all his years as her clerk, he'd been late, what? Twice? Once when Anaya had been born, the second after Hurricane Sandy, when half of their roof had blown off and most of the town had no electricity!

But the last thing Judge Abraham wanted was excuses. "Sorry, Your Honor."

"You look terrible, too," she noted, peering at him through her bifocals. "What did you do, dress in a cave?"

Ah, Judge Abraham. Always the one to dole out compliments. But it was true. He'd been so late that he hadn't had a chance to shave or brush his teeth. Kadir straightened his tie again, as if that would help him look better, and pushed a folder over her grand mahogany desk. "Just saw Judge Gardner in the hall."

He hadn't *just* seen him; he had seen him yesterday, but, well, it was as good an excuse as the judge was going to get. She grunted, not looking up from her paperwork.

"You know he's going on leave next week."

Another grunt. One would think Judge Abraham didn't like Judge Gardner. But did Judge Abraham like anyone? She was always stalking down the halls with a scowl and a massive chip on her shoulder. She scared adults and young children alike. As usual, Kadir allowed the grunts and short temper to roll off his back. He was learning a lot from Judge Abraham, so taking some gruff was worth it for his future career. Kadir hoped one day to become a judge. Even though Judge Abraham was tough to work for, she was known as one of the best, and that was good enough for Kadir.

"He asked me to ask you if you'd be so kind as to take on some of his cases," Kadir said, pushing the folder closer to her so she could no longer ignore it.

Judge Abraham dropped her pen and opened the file with an annoying click of her tongue. "The nerve of that man. As if I don't do enough as it is. Asking me to take over some of his workload just because he's not feeling well!"

Kadir shrugged. "Well, he's having a quadruple bypass ..."

"So? It's his own fault. Gardner swallows food like a garbage truck.

How's that my problem?"

Kadir might as well have said Judge Gardner had a minor scrape on his knee.

Judge Abraham lifted the pages from the file and began to read them. Well, at least she wasn't thinking about his tardiness anymore. No standing in the corner today.

A smile slowly appeared around Judge Abraham's eyes, widening more and more until it took over her face. "Oh, yes. Of course I would like to help Judge Gardner. I'm very happy to take over some of his cases—some more than others."

Kadir froze. What the heck? The judge didn't like anything.

"In fact, I would love to," she said, closing the file and handing it back to Kadir. "Tell Judge Gardner no problem; I got his back."

The judge stood up, straightening her blouse as she reached for the wooden coat rack where her black robe hung. She shrugged into it and, when she next turned, Kadir realized she wasn't just smiling.

The judge was laughing.

Had he ever seen her laugh before?

It wasn't jovial, happy laughter, though. It bordered on evil.

She strode past him, talking and laughing to herself, as Kadir stared after her. The moment the door closed behind her, he opened the file and read down the list of cases.

Then he dropped the file on the desk and scrubbed his stubble-covered face with his hands.

Oh no. This is not good.

CHAPTER 8

Bad News

GWEN PULLED THEIR RAV-4 into the garage and looked over at Dennis as he started to nod off again. She turned the ignition off and jiggled his bony shoulder gently.

"Not yet," she said to him. He might have only been a shadow of his former self, but if she let him fall asleep now, he would be up most of the night.

Dennis started, blinking in the bright fluorescent garage lights, then forced his eyes open. Once again, the chemo was inside him, ravaging his body so it could eventually save him. He clutched at the paper bag he carried during car trips, since the treatments made him sick to his stomach, and his head dropped to the side.

"I think we should go dancing tonight," Dennis said to her with a rakish wink.

Gwen opened the door to the car, stepped out, and looked at him. "I'll have to take a rain check on that, Romeo," she said. She came around to the passenger side, opened the door, and helped him out of the car and up the stairs to the house. There, she helped him to bed, removing his shoes and getting him comfortable.

When Dennis slumped between the pillows, his eyes fastened on a photo of Terrell, the frame atop a piano that was no longer played. This room had once been Gwen's conservatory, but now, it served a more important purpose. "Make sure you call him and tell him I'm fine," Dennis said, his short and tense breaths slowly returning to normal. "You know the boy worries too much. Like you."

"Right. Let us worry. Don't you concern yourself about anything but feeling better," Gwen admonished him.

"I *am* feeling better! Already!" he said brightly, teasing her. "You better get some champagne on ice so we can celebrate. I can show you my dance moves while you play the piano."

Gwen raised an eyebrow, though it was a relief to see him in such good spirits. "You'd better take it easy."

Dennis grinned at her. "When do I ever take things hard? That's you, my dear."

Gwen swallowed. It was true. Dennis was the lighthearted one, the one who always saw the positive side of things. She, like Terrell, was the worrywart, rushing around like a bat out of hell, playing the "What-if" game until it made her sick. "This round of chemo has to work," she said softly, sitting on the edge of his bed. "It just has to."

"It will, it did," Dennis returned, taking her hand and patting it. "Thank you. You're the best thing that's ever happened to me."

Gwen smiled down at him and gave him a soft, chaste kiss on the side of a jaw crusted with silver stubble.

Uncoupling was a good thing. If it hadn't been the law, maybe Dennis would have remained married to that witch of a first wife, and Gwen would never have met him and had twenty-six of the most wonderful years of her life with him. Or maybe none of the laws mattered. Maybe some people were just destined to be together, and human laws didn't make a difference. Maybe she and Dennis would have found each other no matter what. Maybe ...

When she stirred from her thoughts, Gwen realized that Dennis had fallen asleep still holding her hand. She lifted it to her lips and kissed it, whispering, "So much for dancing," and tip-toed out of the room just as her cell phone began to buzz in her pocket.

Gwen saw it was Kadir calling her. *Hmm, wonder what this is about?* thought Gwen. *Maybe something to do with Riya? Maybe she is sick and can't come to work tomorrow.* Gwen had already begun to mentally shuffle around the next day's busy to-do list as she took the call.

"Hey Kadir, what's up? Everything all right?"

"Yes, yes, we're all fine here," he said, leaving Gwen even more nonplussed. Certainly, Kadir wasn't the type to call to shoot the breeze. "I received some information, and I thought I should share."

"All right." Gwen listened as Kadir spilled the news to her, his voice grave. She froze, saying, "Mmmmm," at the appropriate intervals, but all the while, her blood had begun to go cold. When Kadir finished, she pressed her lips together to keep herself from screaming in exasperation. Then Gwen let out a, "Well, I appreciate you letting me know, Kadir."

"Anytime," he responded. "Have a good night."

Gwen ended the call and let out a shrill cry. She couldn't help it.

One thing that Dennis's diagnosis had done was give her a healthy dose of perspective. She'd learned not to sweat the small stuff. Compared to what Dennis was going through, it was all small stuff.

And yes, this was a small issue, but why did it always seem like the man upstairs was trying to make things as hard as possible for her at a time when she really could've used a break?

Gwen made a motion like she was going to throw the phone across the room but caught herself just in time.

"Gwen?"

She clenched her teeth. She'd woken Dennis.

She went back into his room and said, "I'm sorry. Didn't mean to wake you."

"That was Kadir? Is Riya okay?"

Dennis had heard who was on the phone. She nodded. "Judge Gardner is going on leave, so Judge Abraham will be taking over some of his cases, and one of them is the Healys' espouse case."

Dennis studied her silently, waiting for more. "And?"

Gwen threw up her hands. "And what? I don't know what. You know she chews people up and spits them out. And she's worse with me." Gwen vaguely recalled the last time they'd met outside the courthouse. It was two years ago at a benefit, and all the lawyers had chipped in to buy one of the tables. Judge Abraham had given her a head-to-toe icy glare and told her, bluntly, that she'd made the wrong color choice by choosing a yellow gown.

"What am I going to do?" Gwen asked.

Dennis smiled at her. "What do you mean? You do what you always do. You do the absolute best for your clients. You fight for love."

"That's what *you* always did," Gwen reminded him. "Always fighting for love. But I'm not so sure all these people are still in love. And half of the time, I don't know what I'm doing. You remember, I didn't start out as an espouse lawyer. That was your calling. I worked in the corporate world. I didn't deal with any of this family stuff. Remember?"

"Yes, I remember. But you're a good espouse lawyer, Sport."

Sport. That was the nickname Dennis had given her when they'd started dating. It was a joke because Gwen had never been good at anything sporty at all, and she'd always been quite a bad sport whenever she lost a case. "You believe in all this love stuff. I just like to win. That's why I'm so good."

"Hmmm." Dennis's eyebrows crinkled together, giving her his *I'm not sure I totally believe you* look.

She nodded. "Maybe Judge Abraham and I are not as far apart on this uncoupling business as we are with everything else in life. After all, if you and she didn't uncouple, we never would have married or had Terrell."

My life would have been nothing. Gwen stopped herself before saying it out loud and then admonished herself. *Stop with the what-ifs. You sound crazy.*

As if reading her mind, Dennis said, "But we did. And like I said, you're the best thing that ever happened to me. But you know ... it's not for everyone. I know uncoupling is the norm. But some people just belong together. And as their lawyer, you have to believe that the Healys are those people."

Gwen nodded. He yawned, looking tired and sallow. She leaned over and kissed him, promising herself not to wake him again.

No matter how much she dreaded the idea of entering Carly Abraham's courtroom, she would do it. And, as Dennis had said, she would defend the Healys and try to get them what they wanted ... even though she wasn't as sure as Dennis was about espousing.

CHAPTER 9

Are We in Trouble?

GREAT. JUST GREAT, Avery thought as she made her way down the hall of Oldfield Middle School toward the administrative offices. Clutching the pink hall pass, she was happy to have been pulled out of science with grumpy old Mr. Walton, but ... what the heck had she done now?

In the past, yes. Avery had gotten in trouble for chewing gum, for unauthorized cell phone use, and talking ... oh, she was always unable to stop talking to her friends. Some things needed to be said right away, like that James had walked by her in the hall and nodded his head in her direction, or that Mr. Brinkley, their social studies teacher, had a rip in the seam of his pants. Waiting a full forty-five minutes for class to end was just impossible.

But all she'd been doing was sitting slumped in her chair, reading a boring passage from her bio book on regeneration, actually doing what she was supposed to be doing in class. The next thing she knew, Mr. Walton was in front of her, waving the pink slip near her nose.

Wonderful. Her parents would totally ream her if she was in real trouble.

Avery neared the wing that housed attendance, guidance, and the principal's office. The long line of chairs outside was usually reserved for the kids who'd screwed up, and all were empty, save for one seat.

It was occupied by her brother, Sam.

Relief washed over her. If Golden Boy Sam was down here, she couldn't be in trouble. He didn't know the meaning of the word. But no sooner had Avery started to relax when a realization hit her.

"Oh, my God. Do you think something happened to Mom and Dad?"

Her brother's nose was buried in some lame book about pirates. Sam looked up at her glumly. "No."

For the second time, she let out a big rush of air in relief. Avery sat down on the edge of the seat beside him. "Oh. Phew. So ... are we in trouble for something?"

Sam gave her a doubtful look. "Me? In trouble? Please. Teachers love me."

Truth. She wracked her brain, trying to think of what else it could be. "Then what?"

He shrugged. "I don't know. Mrs. Elliot just said that the guidance counselor wanted to talk to us. She said it was not a big deal."

For once, Avery was glad to have a brother who was such a teacher's pet. They told him things, at least, like he was a regular human being. The extent of Avery's conversations with Mrs. Elliot, the principal's administrative assistant, had become a series of grunts and disappointed looks. Elliot pretty much thought Avery was a doofus.

A door opened, and Ms. Kim, the guidance counselor, poked her head out. "Hello, children!" she said brightly.

Ms. Kim was the type of woman who seemed to have more energy than she knew what to do with. Her hair was bright red, curly, and frizzy, and as she bounced over to the kids, pulling her sleeves over the tattoos on her arms, she gave them a look of complete pity. As usual, Ms. Kim was dressed head to toe in one monochrome color. Today that color was blue—blue headband that was doing a poor job of controlling her hair, blue dress cinched at the waist with a blue belt, blue high heels, and blue stockings with sparkles. When the siblings stood up, Ms. Kim wrapped an arm around each of them, drawing them toward her office, almost like the Godmother from *Cinderella* dragging them to get ready for the ball. "Let's get some things done!" she squealed.

"Err … okay," Avery muttered, wondering why everything Ms. Kim said seemed to end in an exclamation point.

Ms. Kim had a thing for smiley faces, too. They were all over her office, an audience of a million smiling faces—mostly yellow—staring down at them. Maybe Ms. Kim thought that in a room filled with smileys, it was impossible to be in a bad mood, but it had the opposite effect on Avery. In fact, it kind of creeped her out.

Avery removed a smiley-face-shaped pillow from the chair—like she wanted a smiley face kissing her butt?—and sat down across the desk from Ms. Kim, Sam beside her. The room also smelled like a jungle, probably because of all the potted plants and wildflowers on the windowsill.

Avery suppressed a sneeze while Ms. Kim laced her fingers in front of her on a bright yellow blotter. Her voice turned somber, dripping with sympathy. "So. Big things going on at home, huh?"

Avery looked past her, up to the "It's a Good Day to Have a Good Day!" poster, which had an explosion of smiling yellow faces all over it. Of course. Of course, that's what this was about. Her parents. The espouse.

The espouse, which, for the past few days, she had managed to put out of her head simply by following these rules: A. Don't think about it. B. Don't talk about it. And C. If anyone tries to talk about it, namely Sam, smack him upside the head.

It had worked well; that is, up until now.

"Yeah," Avery muttered, looking over at Sam, who was playing with a loose thread on the sleeve of his Under Armour sweatshirt.

Lower lip jutting out, Sam nodded with intense vigor. Avery knew that nod. The poor little guy was about two minutes away from pouring out his soul to Ms. Kim and asking her to hold him while he cried. All Ms. Kim had to do was ask him how he felt, and it would be game over. The kid wore his heart, not on his sleeve, but tattooed all over his body, in glowing, fluorescent paint.

"I wanted to talk to you guys about it. This is a safe place, kids. You can come here whenever you want to unload."

No thanks, Avery thought immediately. But Sam leaned forward, ready to spew his thoughts and feelings.

Oh, no. Bio was way more tolerable than this. Suddenly, Avery longed to be back there, listening to Mr. Walton drone on about bacteria.

Avery shuffled in the chair. It was suddenly mega-uncomfortable, making her wish she had kept the smiley face pillow. What could she do? She certainly couldn't smack Ms. Kim upside the head.

"Actually, I'm good," Avery blurted, pointing to the exit. "I'll just ..."

Before she could stand, Sam started to cry, big, blubbering sobs that shook his entire chubby body. "It's like they don't love us any more!"

For all that was good and holy. Avery slumped back and buried her face in her hands as Sam started to spew like a volcano. Sam whimpered on about how he felt like it was his fault, how his parents were so busy talking about getting espoused that they didn't even notice he'd gotten straight As last semester, how in his last soccer game he couldn't concentrate and a grounder went right through his legs. He had a nightmare last night where his parents forgot to pick him up from school. It was all so stream-of-consciousness, Avery could only catch bits and pieces.

When Sam started to bawl into his hands, all Avery could do was stare at the poor creature, wondering how he was even related by blood.

She leaned over to him, a horrified look on her face. She said, "Wait. You're having nightmares?"

Sam sniffled in response. Ms. Kim plucked a tissue out of a smiley-face holder and handed it to Avery as if she was expected to clean up after her little brother.

Avery tucked it into his lap, patted her chest, and looked at Ms. Kim. "Personally, I'm okay. Never better."

Ms. Kim eyed Avery suspiciously. It was clear she didn't believe Avery. "Still, getting espoused is a major change in your life, and it's only natural to experience all kinds of emotions. Uncertainty. Aggression. Depression. Suicidal thoughts?"

Avery stared at her, then at her screen saver, which was flashing beside her. It said, "Happy is as Happy does!" with a giant smiley face bouncing all over the screen. "Nope. I'm good. Happy is as happy does, you know?"

Ms. Kim's suspicion did not soften. "Yes, well. Nonetheless, your parents have communicated their intentions to us, and as educators, we are very invested in your emotional well-being. Therefore, we have a number of programs in place that you'll benefit from."

Sam thanked Ms. Kim. *Prematurely,* Avery thought. If Ms. Kim thought it would help lessen the trauma for them to go swimming with sharks, she got the feeling Sam would be all-in.

Avery shifted in her seat again, something coiling, tight, in the pit of her stomach. "Like what kind of programs?" She could not keep the dread out of her voice.

"Well, there's the Adopt a Teacher program, which would let you have one teacher to talk to, morning or night, whenever you need it. And we will set up weekly appointments with your parents and me so we can ease you into your new life," Ms. Kim said. "Of course, we'll work out the permanent schedules for whoever will be picking you up and on which days, making sure you're all comfortable with the arrangements."

Avery's stomach sank. Her butt hurt more than ever. Nothing about this would ever be comfortable.

"And then, of course, there's COEIP every Wednesday afternoon, right here in the music room. And *moi*," Ms. Kim gleefully said while pointing to herself, "I am the COEIP leader! We have kids from the entire Huntington school district who are going through espouse, and they attend right here at our school. Isn't that wonderful?"

Oh, no no no! Avery clutched her abdomen. She was going to hurl. The Children of Espoused Intervention Program was a self-help group for kids whose parents were going through espouse. One time, Avery and her friend Scarlet had left for cheerleading practice out the music wing doors, which was closest to the football field. They had happened to look in the tiny window of the door to see the COEIP kids sitting in a circle among the empty music stands, *holding hands.*

That was probably the sorriest sight she had ever seen. Scarlet had elbowed her in the ribs and started to sing "Kumbaya." Wasn't that what they did in meetings like that? Discuss feelings, hug, and sing songs?

No thanks. That would not make her feel better as much as make her want to vomit her lunch all over the music wing.

"That's not mandatory, is it?" Avery asked with a raised eyebrow.

Ms. Kim looked disappointed. "Well, no. But it's encouraged."

"I'll go," Sam offered.

Of course, he would. Groups like that were simply made for people like Sam. Avery gave him a sideways glance. *Little brown-noser.*

"Yeah, I mean, I would, but I have cheerleading," Avery explained with a shrug.

Ms. Kim went to her computer and clicked her fingers along the keyboard. She studied the screen. "Says here cheerleading practice starts at four. The COEIP meetings are at three-thirty. You're in luck."

Right. I'm so lucky, Avery thought. "Great," she muttered. *Scarlet will have a field day with this one.*

Ms. Kim said, "Now Avery. No attitude."

Avery forced a smile. "Attitude? What attitude? I seriously can't wait," she said in sarcastic mock-brightness. She lifted her fringed purse onto her shoulder. "Are we done here?"

She stood up and looked at Sam, who seemed rooted in his seat, waiting for his hug from Ms. Kim. Rolling her eyes, she stepped toward the door, expecting Ms. Kim to tell her to stop.

But Ms. Kim simply stood up and went to the door, holding it open for her. She reached out and gave her shoulder a tight squeeze. "Remember, Avery. If you need anything ... sometimes it really does help to talk these things out."

Talk? About her parents? That was the last thing she wanted to do. Now that the door was open, Avery could see students filling the halls, shuttling between classes. That meant bio was over, so it was on to gym class. Funny, she hadn't even heard the bell ring. Avery scurried out of the office, leaving Ms. Kim to give Sam a huge hug.

And now everyone would see Sam and her coming out of the guidance counselor's office. Of course, that would get the gossip mills working overtime. Avery already knew they were whispering about her, thanks to that bratty Cara, Sam's friend, who never met a secret she could keep. The only good thing about Cara was her brother, James. *Just perfect.*

"Uh-huh," Avery muttered to herself, trying to fall in line with the crowd of kids as if nothing were wrong. She still had to get to her locker to get her gym bag.

"Hey, you," a voice called behind her.

Every hair on the back of her neck stood at attention. Avery knew that voice.

She whirled around so fast that she nearly lost balance, trying to plaster her most fetching smile onto her face. "Oh, hi, James."

James sauntered toward her, one hand in his pocket, pencil behind his ear, notebook in his hand, cool as always. "I never see you around here this time of day."

True, Avery was usually on the other side of the building in the average kid's classrooms. But today, she had had to go to the guidance counselor's office due to her selfish, silly parents. James was in honors classes, so she rarely bumped into him, except at lunch. "Yeah, well ..."

James pointed behind him toward the offices. "Did I just see you come out of Ms. Kim's?"

Avery started to shake her head but gave up halfway through. She had the feeling he could see right through her anyway. Besides, James knew about the espouse, and it hadn't made things weird between them yet. "Yeah." She shrugged. "My parents are officially freaks, and therefore, I have to pay the price. It sucks."

He nodded understandingly. "Hey. Where are you off to?"

"My locker. Then gym."

"I have study hall next. Can I walk with you?"

A little part of Avery's heart melted right there. Her breath hitched, and her palms slickened. "Um. Sure."

As they walked together, Avery felt like she was in one of her dreams. In her dreams, they were always in these dull, brown hallways surrounded by rows and rows of tan lockers, but he would reach for her hand and hold it. Everything would brighten as if encased in an ethereal halo of light. Other students would zoom past them, but it was like they could see only each other. Her chest stuttered at the thought.

Then Avery blinked and found an awkward silence stretching between them. She realized he had asked her something and was waiting for a response. "Err ... what?"

James stopped to high-five another eighth grader. "I just asked how things were going?"

"Oh ... good," Avery said. Right now, things were very, very good. Perfect. A dream come true. She smiled at him. "Great. Why do you ask?"

His eyebrows narrowed. "With your parents?"

Oh. Oh, right. That. Suddenly, nausea began to bubble up in her throat again. Avery frowned. "No," she admitted. "That sucks."

"Ah." James nodded. "You know, if you ever want to, you know ..."

Avery looked up at him gratefully. *When had he gotten so tall?* It had been such a long time since they'd been this close. She took a deep breath.

And then, just like that, it was as if a dam broke.

"I don't understand why my parents are doing this. They always argue about the stupidest things! And they pretty much lead separate lives as it is. Dad's always working, and Mom is always dealing with us. It's like they don't seem to get that being espoused means you're going to be stuck with one another. Like they're living in an alternate universe or something. And what I don't get is ..."

Avery stopped when she realized they were standing in front of her locker, and James was staring intently, nodding as if he was trying to process all the words pouring from her mouth. *Geez, maybe I am related to Sam after all.*

Avery tucked a lock of long blond hair behind her ear and bit her lip nervously. "I'm sorry. I didn't mean to unload on you like that."

James shook his head. "No. No. Whatever. I mean, it's fine." One side of James's mouth quirked up. "I like listening to you talk."

Avery's eyes widened. "You do?" She stopped when she realized she looked like a puppy, lapping at his heels. James probably thought she never got compliments from guys. "I mean, thanks. I like talking to you, too."

James grinned at her and ran his hand through his shaggy hair, momentarily disrupting the pencil that had been lost behind his ear. It rolled away, and he leaned down to pick it up. "Then we should do it more often. Later, Ave."

James started to walk away, and Avery stared after him, her blood pulsing furiously through her veins. *Who knew?* Ms. Kim was right. Talking about it *definitely* had her feeling better, though not for the reasons Ms. Kim would think.

When he was out of view, Avery turned back to her locker, twisting in the combination. She pulled the door open and reached for her phone on the top shelf. She was just thumbing to Scarlet, *OMG you'll never guess what happened!* when the bell rang.

Fantastic. She definitely heard that one, and it meant she was late. Crazy late.

That would mean detention. Her parents would kill her. Or maybe she could wrangle a little guilt out of them because of the espouse, and they would let her slide? One of the benefits of espoused parents!

CHAPTER 10

Who Is the Grown-Up?

DRIED LEAVES FELL OVER THE CAR as Kadir drove his daughter down Old Field Road toward the middle school in his 2009 Volvo.

He checked the clock on the dash. He had a trial to prepare for and didn't want to be late for the fourth time, especially so soon. If he didn't hurry, and if drop-off wasn't smooth, he'd be cutting it close.

A car in front of him constantly used its brakes, and Kadir shook a fist at him. "Jackass!" he hissed under his breath.

"Dad!" came the voice from the back seat.

He looked in the rear-view mirror at the daughter he was chauffeuring. Anaya was reading, this time, *Animal Farm*. Guilt washed over him; Riya would've killed him for cursing in front of Anaya. Kadir had practically forgotten she was there.

Fourteen now and Anaya still refused to sit in the front passenger seat. Kadir wanted her to, but no. Other parents had told him it was a big rite of passage that in New York, once a child hit the recommended age of twelve, they could finally move into the front seat. Most kids begged for the chance. But Anaya? She'd never been interested in sitting up front. She'd always wanted the back. "I'm small for my age, Dad," she'd said, "and it's safer. It just makes sense."

That was Anaya, his sensible girl.

His own bright, wonderful, sensitive daughter. And Kadir had forgotten her. *Talk about a jackass.*

"Sorry," he said, taking his aluminum travel mug of coffee from the center console and sipping it. "You finish all your homework?"

Anaya looked up from her book only to roll her eyes at him.

Of course, she had. Anaya was the type of girl who worked a chapter ahead. That was a stupid thing to ask. He tried again. "Anything new happening at school?"

She shrugged, and he thought it was another dead end. As he scraped the deepest corners of his mind to think of another suitable topic of conversation, she said, "The Healys are getting espoused."

Kadir raised an eyebrow. Of course, she must have heard it from Avery. They were friends. "How did you know about that? Did Avery tell you?"

Anaya shook her head.

"You're still friends, right?"

"Yes. Kind of, but she has other friends now," she muttered. "But I heard Sam say it the other day when we were waiting to be picked up."

They arrived in front of the stately school, the front of which reminded Kadir of a brick version of jail. Well, they hadn't quite arrived in front. No, there was a long line of cars clogging the drop-off lane, spilling out onto the main road.

Perfect. Kadir craned his head to see that the moron in a gray BMW had double-parked to go into the school. *Really?* It was late October, which should have been plenty of time for people to grasp the complexities of school drop-off—which was so ridiculously easy it boggled the mind how people kept screwing it up. Was this crap still going to be going on in June?

Probably.

The cars in front advanced at a snail's pace. A lurch forward, followed by brake lights, lurch, brake, lurch, brake. Kadir kept right on the bumper of the car in front of him. "And how do you feel about that?"

Anaya shrugged. "Um. I don't know. Fine I guess."

Kadir didn't buy that. Anaya was serious like him, but she was opinionated, like Riya. There were few things she didn't have a theory on.

"It's okay," he said, trying to sound gentle, even though yet another parent ahead had decided to park in the middle of the drop-off lane and start a conversation with one of the teachers. "Really. You can tell me. I noticed that you seemed a little on edge during the uncoupling discussion."

She cleared her throat, then looked down at her book sheepishly. "I know."

"And? You don't want us to get uncoupled?"

Anaya shook her head.

Kadir glanced at her as he rolled forward, his gaze lingering a second too long so that he had to jam on his brake to avoid rear-ending the car in front of him, which had one of those obnoxious *Proud Parent of an Oldfield Middle School Honors Student* bumper stickers on it. "Why is that?"

"Because I think you still love each other. And I like the way things are. Why do they have to change?"

He inhaled sharply. Of course, Anaya was his sensitive little girl.

But more than that, she hated things to change. She didn't want to grow up or move on. His Peter Pan girl.

"All right. But you know, it's not like we still won't love each other. Of course, we will. We'll just be living apart and having two separate places to live, and—"

"And never seeing each other again, pretty much," Anaya muttered, shutting her book and tucking it into the top of her bulging, heavy-duty backpack.

"No, that's ..."

"It's okay, I get it. I know, you're supposed to uncouple. That's the way things are." She slipped her backpack onto her small back. "Anyway, Avery and Sam are pretty bummed about their parents' espouse, and I guess they should be. Now they won't have two Christmases or more parents or even more independence. They're all upset about it."

The car in front of him advanced, and he trailed it, bringing his car safely into the drop-off zone. "But wouldn't you be upset if we decided to espouse?" he asked her, desperate to hear her answer.

But she just shrugged. "I guess that's not supposed to happen. And I'm just a kid, so what do I know? Bye, Dad."

Anaya threw open the door, stepping her bony frame out of the car, and slammed it before he could tell her he loved her. Kadir watched her run toward the front doors, her long black ponytail bouncing behind her. He wondered what the hell that meant.

Are all women this hard to read or just the ones I live with?

Just then, a car horn blared behind Kadir, causing him to jump. He realized that he was now blocking the way. He punched on the gas and drove out of the parking lot, checking the clock on his dash as he sailed onto Old Field Road.

Damned if he was going to be late again.

CHAPTER 11

Friends

JESSICA BAUM SIPPED her Starbucks chai latte and smiled at her ex appreciatively. The adage about absence making the heart grow fonder was true. Michael was more handsome now. Not handsome in a way that made her want him back, but she no longer wanted to smack his face every time she saw him.

That was what you called progress.

It had only been six months since her uncoupling from Michael, but it was, without a doubt, the best thing that had ever happened. In those six months, she'd really grown, opening new doors, doing things that she would never have done had she still been married.

Like Marco.

Marco, the Brazilian pediatrician who had just signed on at the practice where she took the kids.

Marco was something else. She'd taken Cara, who had headaches, into the pediatric offices of Johnson and Brinkman, and their newest addition, Marco Vasil, flirted with Jessica the entire time. She'd left with his phone number, discreetly written on the back of the card for the follow-up appointment.

Michael was wearing an all-black Hugo Boss T-shirt with matching black Vans and a pair of butt-hugging Levi's. The tiredness in his face and the potbelly were both gone, replaced by the look Michael had had when Jessica first set eyes on him in college. Jessica had heard Michael was dating a blonde ten years his junior. Obviously, it agreed with him.

Jessica and Michael usually met on Sundays, which was when they traded the kids off. Since their homes were in the same school district, it was easy: the kids spent one week with Jessica and then one week with Michael. Every Sunday afternoon, they would get together and fill each other in on the goings-on of their children before they switched the kids.

It was a perfect arrangement, all planned during the uncoupling process.

James and Cara were sitting at a nearby table, playing with their electronics, earbuds fastened in their ears, dead to the world. Even so, Jessica leaned in and whispered, "Just so you know, Cara got her first period."

Michael looked up from his phone. "What?"

"You know, her—"

"But she's only eleven." He said it as if Jessica had just announced his daughter had grown a horn in the center of her head.

"Yes. But it's well within the—"

"Does she still have it?" Michael was staring at Cara now like she was an alien who had just entered the coffee shop and announced plans to devour them.

"Yes, but it's okay. She has extra pads, so she'll be fine."

He was still studying her doubtfully. That was one thing that Jessica didn't miss about Michael. All things female, he was completely lost on. That's why she'd found Marco so refreshing. He didn't shy away from those things like some bashful twelve-year-old boy.

Jessica took a sip from her latte and looked up as she spied a familiar couple outside the shop window. "Look who it is," Jessica murmured.

Michael turned. "Oh, hell. Have you talked to her lately?"

"Not lately. Not since two weeks ago when I tried to talk her out of it. But you know Sara. She's a Taurus. A stubborn bull. You can't talk her out of anything," Jessica mumbled as the Healys walked in, Tom shaking the rain from his umbrella. Jessica waved them over.

"Hi!" Sara said, looking genuinely excited to see them as they exchanged kisses all around. "It's great to see you two ... but together?"

Jessica's eyes widened. "Oh, no," she said, as if Sara was suggesting something absurd, like *Does this mean you two are thinking of espousing?* While it wasn't completely unheard of for people who uncoupled to want to recouple, it rarely happened. Why? Because uncoupling worked. It made sense. "We usually get together on Sundays to exchange the kids."

"Oh!" Sara said, face flushing. "Of course."

Sara should have known about the uncoupled kids' schedule even if she was considering espouse. They'd barely talked over the past few months since Jessica and Michael uncoupled, and not at all since Sara had shot down Jessica's hundredth attempt to get her to see how ridiculous espousing was. Conversations with her best friend had quickly gone from easy and fun to feeling like Jessica was banging her head against a wall.

Sara pulled off her raincoat and sat down as Tom went up to the counter to order for the two of them. Jessica silently critiqued Sara's outfit—*same old twinset cashmere cardigan and wool pants. And that hair—God! Didn't she want to cover those roots?* Truthfully, Sara was the last person Jessica could think of who would go against norms and espouse.

"And how are things going with uncoupling?" inquired Sara.

"No complaints," Michael volunteered, grinning from ear to ear. "I heartily recommend it."

Jessica looked over at him. Yes, Michael seemed as happy as the cat who got the cream, but he didn't have to be *that* excited to have gotten rid of her. Jessica cleared her throat. "Yes. It really is a refreshing change of pace," she said brightly. "Helps you to put things in perspective. Reach beyond your comfort zone. When you do, you find out there's a whole vast world out there you haven't explored or that you'd forgotten about since you were single!"

Tom came by, balancing two black coffees and a little Danish with red fruit in the center, which he sweetly placed in front of Sara. Then he went over to James and Cara to give them each a hug.

"What's up, you two?" he said to them before sitting down with the adults.

Jessica smiled. Tom, lean and lanky, always smiling goofily, was like the Pied Piper, the one the kids gravitated to. Jessica sometimes thought if Tom and Sara had uncoupled, they could have simply switched husbands. The four of them got along famously, first when they were all attending Hofstra together, as maid of honor and best man in each other's weddings, and later, when they were just starting their families.

"How are you guys?" Tom asked, sipping his coffee. Jessica noticed the barista had written *Thom* on it.

Who in their right mind spelled Tom like Thom? "Never better," Jessica said, with a glance at her ex. Obviously, Michael was doing well—he looked slimmer, tanned, healthier. But Jessica wasn't so sure the uncoupling had had the same effect on her. Too many romantic dinners with Marco at expensive restaurants had her pants fitting a little more tightly. She leaned in. "So, your big date is coming up, huh?"

Sara pressed her lips together. "Jessica, I told you. We're espousing."

Jessica looked around, startled. Sara said it loudly, too loudly, as if she was proud of it. All around them, there were uncoupled people, meeting new dates, or to exchange kids. And yet Sara just waltzed in and spoke the E-word as loud as could be, with no shame whatsoever. Jessica put a finger to her lips. "Sara, please. Shhh."

Tom shrugged. "What difference does it make? Soon everyone is going to know anyway."

For once, Jessica was glad her kids had those buds in their ears and couldn't hear a thing. Two women in yoga pants, behind Sara, looked at her and whispered to one another, and Jessica could read the word *espouse*, but nothing else. Their lips curled in disgust.

Michael shook his head at Tom. "You're out of your mind, man. You don't know what you're missing, and you are going to put yourself and your kids in a difficult situation."

Tom played with the collar of his polo shirt as he gazed at his wife. "Everyone keeps telling us that. But you know what? I'd miss Sara more."

Jessica stared at them, a sour feeling inside her. *Were they actually ... holding hands under the table? How revolting.*

While Jessica would have loved to stay close to Tom and Sara, it was things like this that made it difficult since they now lived different types of lives. She'd worked tirelessly to convince Sara that espousing was a mistake and yet everything she said just seemed to bounce off like Sara was clad in a suit of cashmere-twinset armor. And now they were here, mooning over each other like two lovestruck teenagers? Jessica wanted to grab her best friend and shake some sense into her.

Sara said, "Our first hearing is Tuesday morning."

Jessica looked over at her kids. *Wow, I always knew Sara was the crazy one, but she was really going through with it.* "That soon, huh?"

Sara nodded as she took a bite of her Danish. It left a little raspberry smear on her lower lip, and Tom promptly wiped it away with the pad of his thumb. Jessica straightened as she noticed an old lady who was studying Sara and Tom. *How embarrassing. Why didn't he just lick it off while he was at it?*

The old lady stood, tied her clear rain-scarf onto her head, and bustled around scattered chairs. She leaned in to them and softly said, "Many years ago, I got espoused. Worse decision I ever made. Don't try to fight the natural order of life! You will only regret it." Then she continued walking out the door.

Tom's mouth opened in confused disbelief, while Sara's face went ashen. She cleared her throat.

"I'm glad we ran into you here," Sara said, more softly now. She glanced at Tom, who nodded encouragingly. "We wanted to let you know that if you don't want to associate with us ..." Sara swallowed. "Now that we are going to espouse, we'll understand."

Jessica's brow wrinkled. "What do you mean?"

But the truth was, she knew exactly what Sara meant. Jessica used to see or text with Sara every day. Now, it was lucky if they bumped into one another ... like today. There was a definite wedge being driven between them.

And though Jessica knew it was partly her doing, she really couldn't bring herself to care. After all, she'd warned Sara that getting espoused was a bad idea. Couples who were so ingrained in one another didn't have lives outside of their own togetherness and found it difficult to associate with those who uncoupled and lived differently.

Tom shrugged, nodding his head in the direction of the yoga-pants-wearing women. "Well, you see it. People have strong feelings when it comes to espouse. They take sides. Uncoupleds tend to stay with uncoupleds."

"And it makes sense," Sara chimed in. "People don't know how to invite us out to places as a couple since most are single, and of course, the number of invitations will drop off because the conversations aren't around single life like, 'Who are you dating?' 'Have you put your profile on that new dating app, DeTach?' So, if you don't want anything to do with us, we'll understand."

Jessica nodded seriously at her friend. Then she smiled. "I'm sorry, but you can't get rid of us that easily."

Yes, you can.

"Yeah man," Michael added. "Are you kidding? Nothing between us will change. We've got your back."

The clouds lifted from Sara's face. She clutched at her chest. "Really? Oh, I'm so relieved!"

Jessica wanted to grab for her hand; if only it wasn't under the table firmly planted in Tom's. Instead, she reached limply out to Sara across the glossy counter. "Of course! You and I have been friends since freshman year at Hofstra! You don't throw that away so easily. We'll always be friends."

Sara nodded, beaming. "I was worried. I know, people will talk. And they will gawk. And I just don't want this to be uncomfortable for you."

Definitely uncomfortable. If they think this is a good idea, they're idiots. But I'm not going to tell them that again. I've already done that a hundred times. Jessica began to lie and started to say, through gritted teeth, that it wouldn't be uncomfortable, when Cara called, "Mo-om!" in that annoying singsong that all kids seemed to know.

Jessica looked at her daughter, who now had her earbuds out, and said tersely, "What?"

"Can Dad take us to his house now?" she complained. "I'm not *feeling* well."

Sara's eyes widened knowingly, "Oh! Has she ..."

Jessica nodded solemnly and rolled her eyes, grabbing for her purse. "Yes. If there's anything worse than a drama queen, it's a drama queen with cramps. We've got to go. It's time to make the switch."

Truthfully, she wasn't in as much of a rush as she made herself out to be, throwing on her jacket and ushering her family out the door. Once she handed the kids off to Michael, she was free and could stay there in Starbucks with her poor, misguided friends, sipping chai lattes as long as she pleased. That freedom was the beauty of uncoupling, even if her friends couldn't see it.

But Jessica had to go. She had a pediatrician waiting for her.

CHAPTER 12

Advice From a Friend

RIYA PRACTICALLY SLEEPWALKED through her duties the entire morning, taking Dennis's vitals, changing his bed linens, setting out his breakfast, putting together the cocktail of pills he had to take. All she could think about was Kadir. Was he really that blind? Did he not see what he was doing to her? Or did he not care?

"Riya," Dennis said sleepily from the bed as she dropped a little paper cup with his morning pills into his palm. "I trust that you're looking out for what's best for me, but is it possible you've forgotten something?"

Riya startled, confused. She did her job well, efficiently, and never forgot anything, especially since in her line of work, this type of error could be the difference between life and death.

She followed Dennis's line of sight to the paper cup and counted the pills. There were only two, which was ...

Not correct. Riya had only given him the anti-nausea and constipation medicine, completely forgetting his immunotherapy pills. *Idiot!*

"Oh, my goodness, Mr. Stevens," said Riya, shamefaced, "I'm so sorry; I don't know where my mind was."

He smiled. "It's because I work you too hard. You're here nearly every day. You should get some rest."

Riya sighed as she hurried back to the kitchen, where the rows of amber bottles were kept. She got the correct dosage and returned to Dennis, checking and rechecking herself. "And miss seeing you? Ha."

Although, she wasn't sure she was much of a nurse after this mindless mistake. How could she have been so careless?

Dennis patted her hand as he took the medicine. "My wife can look after me for one day."

Riya pressed her lips together. "She has a lot on her mind, too. Is the room cold?" She made a move to get him an extra blanket.

Dennis waved her away. "I'm fine. So, does this have to do with your upcoming uncoupling?"

Riya's eyes widened. "How did you guess?"

"I'm an espouse lawyer ... or at least I used to be one. You've been married almost fourteen years, so uncoupling is coming up. And those who want to espouse ... seem to get more stressed."

Riya nodded and slumped against the bed. "Well, yes. I thought Kadir would at least bring up the subject of getting espoused, but he's just proceeding along like the uncoupling is going to happen. I can't believe it. He doesn't even seem to want to discuss it."

"Have you brought it up to him?"

Riya sighed. "Indirectly. He keeps avoiding the subject. You can't legally espouse unless both parties are in full agreement. I could contest the uncoupling, but if Kadir doesn't want to espouse, I not only don't want to force him, but I don't want to put Anaya through unnecessary discomfort having her live in a house with one parent not wanting to be there. The final uncoupling document is all filled out. It just needs to be mailed."

Dennis nodded gravely. "You are married, dear," he said. "Maybe you should be ... I don't know. More *direct*?"

Riya inhaled sharply. Yes, she and Kadir used to talk about everything. Why not this? The deadline was coming soon. Everyone knew that once the final uncoupling document was mailed, there was no turning back. It'd be sent to the government, processed, and in six months, the final uncoupling documents would arrive. That would be the end of their marriage.

Riya's heart physically hurt at the thought. She and Kadir had been high school sweethearts. He was all she'd ever known, and she, all he'd ever known. Maybe that was why the thought of moving on to someone else scared her so much. But it didn't just scare her ... she dreaded it.

Riya blinked out of her thoughts to see Dennis smiling reassuringly at her. Her cheeks flushed. He was supposed to be the patient, and yet just now, she had the feeling he was the one taking care of her.

She straightened the blouse of her hospital scrubs and moved to refill the glass of water at his bedside when he grabbed her hand and held it.

"Don't worry, Riya," Dennis said to her, his voice strong and direct. "I've been in the marriage-saving business for a long time. And I promise you, love will make everything work out. You'll see."

Riya smiled weakly at him. *I'm sure love would make everything work out, but both people have to be in love.*

She wasn't so sure Kadir loved her anymore.

CHAPTER 13

The Good Judge

GWEN SMILED AT THE COUPLE seated beside her. It had been one year, one full year of paperwork, of waiting, of court appearances, of more waiting ... but now, the day was finally here.

Edward and Joelle Norton were one step away from the final ruling ... espoused in the eyes of the law.

"So, after this, we've done it?" Joelle leaned over and asked her, for what had to be the fifth time over the past five minutes.

Gwen understood. After fighting for something for so long, jumping through hoop after hoop, it was hard to believe that this process had an end. She nodded. "We just have to receive the final ruling from Judge Gardner."

Joelle leaned back and nodded, gnawing on her lip. Edward reached over and took her hand as Judge Gardner entered from his chambers and proceeded to climb with an effort to the bench. At one point, he stopped to steady himself against the rail, and the bailiff stood to help, but Judge Gardner waved the bailiff away and made it to the front of his desk. Gwen looked at Robert Feinstein, the state prosecutor, across the aisle, who gave her an expression that said, "It's a shame, we're losing one of our best."

Judge Gardner was Gwen's favorite. He was a fair, good man who'd been espoused himself many years ago. His wife of forty-five years had passed on about a year ago, and lately, he'd complained of chest pains, discovering he had heart artery blockages that required surgery. He was a little pale and frail, and Gwen was surprised he was still handling cases and not confined to a hospital bed.

Judge Gardner plopped into his chair and looked at the docket in front of him. "Mrs. Stevens," he said kindly to Gwen. "Are your clients ready to start?"

"Yes, Your Honor." Gwen motioned for them to stand.

Judge Gardner spoke to Gwen's clients. "State your names, please."

Only a few more minutes, thought Gwen.

"In the case of Joelle and Edward Norton v the State of New York," the judge said, lifting his gavel. The two lovebirds held their breath, but Gwen didn't. She'd done many cases before Judge Gardner, and this one was a done deal. "The court declares you two espoused in the eyes of the law. You'll receive the written judgment as well as the espouse decree in the mail between four to six weeks' time."

He slammed the gavel down.

Edward and Joelle hugged each other, then turned over the low railing and hugged their two children. Gwen smiled at them. "Congratulations, you two. Go somewhere tonight to celebrate."

"Oh, we will," Edward said with tears in his eyes, shaking her hand.

Joelle tried to thank Gwen, too, but she was held speechless by the flow of tears.

Gwen held up a hand. "Please. Don't thank me for doing my job."

She looked over at Judge Gardner. "May I approach the bench, Your Honor?"

"Of course, Mrs. Stevens," he said kindly, motioning her up like an old grandfather offering a treat to a child.

Gwen strode forward, her heels—the only pair she owned—clicking on the wood floor. "I just wanted to wish you the best for your surgery and a speedy recovery. We'll all miss you here."

Robert Feinstein was packing up his briefcase and overheard the conversation. "Ditto!" he said, waving at the judge.

"Thank you, and I hope Dennis gets back on his feet as well. I miss having him here too," Judge Gardner said with a grateful smile.

Gwen thanked him, then packed up her things and started to leave the courtroom. When she reached the door, Feinstein was waiting for her. "I guess I'll see you tomorrow? The Healy case? I've been assigned to that one."

Gwen groaned inwardly. She was trying to put all thoughts of that case out of her mind. It should have been routine. But with Judge Abraham at the bench, it would be like navigating a minefield in the dark. "Oh, yes. I look forward to it."

About as much as I look forward to having my yearly pap smear.

"Well, it won't be the same around here with Judge Gardner away, that's for sure," Robert said.

They walked into the rotunda, which was swarming with people letting out for lunch. Gwen shrugged. "I suppose. Judge Abraham is definitely ... a personality."

Feinstein let out a loud, goofy guffaw, and for a second, Gwen thought he was having a coughing fit or choking on something. *Haw-haw-haw.* Feinstein was one of those people who thought he was extra charming but had a bit of a clumsy side, like Goofy, pretending to be James Bond. He said, "She does have a strong one, that's for sure. But I like that spark, that feistiness."

Gwen stared at him, unable to believe that there was anything *likable* about Judge Abraham. Her stomach churned. Of course, she must have had some good qualities or Dennis would never have married her. But Gwen was under the impression that she'd lost them all after the uncoupling. "Well, yes, that's one way of putting it. I prefer to think of her more as nasty than feisty."

Feinstein turned to her, realization washing over him. "Oh, right. I seem to remember you have some connection with the judge?"

Gwen nodded. "Judge Abraham uncoupled from my husband."

That loud cough of a guffaw, again, *Haw-haw-haw.* "Right!" He dropped his briefcase on a bench and donned his long black raincoat. "There's always something. Never a dull moment in court, huh?"

Gwen knew that. For all the dull sameness, there was always something to spark things up. And tomorrow, there would be Judge Carly Abraham. Truthfully, Gwen would have preferred the dullness to the Wicked Witch of the Bench.

"Judge Abraham's a lovely woman," Feinstein said, pushing open the door to the courthouse, leaving Gwen staring at him, mouth agog.

Lovely? The woman has claws and fangs. As far as Gwen could tell, there was absolutely nothing lovely about her. Gwen had always admired Robert Feinstein. She had met him a number of times through Dennis. He'd been a fixture at the courthouse for many years and a good, fair man with a sterling reputation.

She'd never realized until this moment that he was also insane.

CHAPTER 14

First Court Appearance

GWEN WOKE THE FOLLOWING MORNING with a pit of dread in her stomach. Despite a "knock 'em dead" pep-talk from Dennis, she'd only felt worse as she made her way into the courthouse.

When she arrived, Sara and Tom Healy were standing in the rotunda, waiting for her, as previously arranged. Gwen plastered on a smile, trying to project confidence.

"Well," she explained to them as she led them into the courtroom and sat down at the defense table. "This first hearing is usually just a ten-minute thing. It's usually the easiest of all the proceedings, where I'll just announce that we're submitting for irreconcilable concurrence and ask for a waiver of the six-month trial separation so we can get this fast-tracked. You will still be expected to attend uncouple counseling, which is standard procedure for espouse. And we will be done for today."

They nodded. Gwen had explained this to them before, but from her experience, most couples found the repetition reassuring.

"Also, in the interest of speeding things up, I'm going to ask for a waiver of the court-appointed counselor for the children. I'll also ask to get a forensic accountant assigned to the case immediately to begin the process of selling your second house to pay any taxes you may owe."

"And this is normal, right?" Tom asked.

Gwen nodded. "Yes. It's called no-fault espouse."

Sara tittered nervously. "It's so confusing."

"Actually, ever since New York became a no-fault espouse state, most judges are more lenient with rules. There are still quite a lot of hoops, but if things go our way, a lot fewer of them. Again, all standard procedure," Gwen whispered as she heard Feinstein drop his briefcase on the prosecutor table to her right.

Gwen looked over at him. "Counselor," she said with a nod.

"Counselor." Feinstein nodded back and slipped into his seat while adjusting his expensive black suit.

A couple of minutes later, Kadir walked into the courtroom, dropped a file on the judge's bench, and smiled at Gwen as he walked over toward his seat near the bailiff, who stood and said, "All rise."

Everyone shuffled to their feet.

Judge Abraham swept into the room, lugging that massive chip on her shoulder. Her white-blond hair had been "done up" into a hairspray helmet, and she was wearing light pink lipstick that did not match her fiery temper. A frown deeply etched on her face, she slumped into her chair and looked over her bifocals at the people in the courtroom as if they'd personally offended her.

Then her eyes fell on Gwen, and a sadistic smile spread across the judge's face.

Gwen knew right then that she was done for. She fought the urge to roll her eyes and mutter under her breath. It would only make things worse.

Judge Abraham picked up the file in front of her, opened it, and lifted a paper. "Case number 200135," she said. "Thomas and Sara Healy v the State of New York. Thomas and Sara Healy are filing a petition to be *espoused*."

Judge Abraham said the last word like it was a dirty slur, then looked up, disgusted, sizing up the couple beside Gwen as if they were two hardened criminals.

Great. If there is anything worse than Judge Abraham, it's Judge Abraham in a nasty mood.

"Are you the Healys?" she spat out, pointing at them as if to accuse them.

They looked at each other, smiling, and nodded.

"Congratulations," she snapped.

Gwen had argued very few cases in front of Judge Abraham. Two, before this one, to be precise. Neither of them had been a fun experience. In the first, the judge had ordered a trial separation without hesitancy, and Gwen had been too green in espouse law to argue the case very well. Eventually, the couple had been granted the espouse, but not until Judge Abraham had made the husband and wife follow every rule and regulation on the books. The poor people; it had taken nearly five years, all of Gwen's patience, and a lot of money. In the second case, Judge Abraham had given her such a hard time during the couple's first appearance that they had had second thoughts and decided to uncouple after all. She could still recall the judge's glee over that; it was as if she actually enjoyed making Gwen miserable.

Gwen wasn't going to let that happen again. Come hell or high water, she was ready to dig in and hold her ground.

Gwen rose to her feet and said, "Yes, Your Honor," the bile thick in her throat. The last thing she wanted to do was "Your Honor" Carly Abraham. "And we would like to file the following petitions—"

"Oh, really? Is that what you would like to do, Ms. Stevens?" Judge Abraham snapped, looking down the long, pointed end of her nose at her. "Last time I checked, this was my courtroom, so I'll be letting you know the procedure. And I didn't ask you to speak. If I have a question, I'll ask it."

Gwen felt her face heating. Next to her, the Healys straightened, like schoolchildren trying to be on their best behavior. Tom cleared his throat.

"Sit down, *Ms.* Stevens." Judge Abraham said it slowly, carefully enunciating the *Ms.*

So, there it was. Carly Abraham might be a judge, but it was clear she wasn't going to play this fair.

Gwen thought for a moment about what Dennis had said to her before she left. *Give 'em hell.* Give his ex-wife hell. And Gwen intended to. Didn't matter whose courtroom it was. She wasn't going to let this witch of a woman treat her clients unfairly while walking over her. "Yes … I understand this is your courtroom, but if it will please the court, this is your very basic espouse case, and since we are now a no-fault espouse state, we can forgo all the extra work …"

"Shut up, *Ms.* Stevens. SHUT. UP." Judge Abraham's voice boomed like thunder. She banged the gavel in a murderous way.

Gwen could do nothing but freeze, a chill snaking its way up her spine. The room was as still and silent as a morgue. No one dared even breathe.

It was only when she'd fallen to her chair with an ungraceful, gobsmacked thud that the astonishment began to morph. It started out as humiliation, a wound to her pride, then indignation. When Judge Abraham turned to address Robert Feinstein, a white-hot rage bubbled inside Gwen so that she could barely sit still.

"Mr. Feinstein, do you have everything in order? Are the Healys up-to-date with their uncoupling finances, child visitation, and yearly uncoupling documents?" the judge asked.

Gwen couldn't help but notice that the judge's voice softened considerably when she spoke to the state prosecutor. Did she like him that much? Or did she just hate Gwen so much more?

"Yes," Mr. Feinstein answered. "Everything is in perfect order. If I may address the defendant counsel's point, however ..."

"No, you may not," Judge Abraham interjected bluntly. She held the paper in front of her as Gwen stole a look at Kadir. He was sitting at his bench beside Vanessa, the bailiff, one hand to his chin and staring at the judge, looking as shell-shocked as Gwen felt. "Now, this is what we're going to do."

She's addressing us like we're children, Gwen thought, flattening her hands out on the table in front of her. If she allowed them to ball into fists, she couldn't trust herself not to come out swinging. Gwen pressed her lips together so her tongue wouldn't get her into trouble. *How infuriatingly condescending this woman is!*

"This is going to follow standard espouse proceedings." Gwen narrowed her eyes at the judge. Gwen shouldn't have dared to hope that Carly Abraham could behave and treat her with a modicum of respect. "That means, *Ms.* Stevens ... that the Healys are going to have to follow the rules as set forth by the State. So, I'm ordering a six-month trial separation, the children will have counseling through the COEIP, and the Healys will attend uncouple counseling. During this time, visitation schedules will need to be strictly followed, the schools will need to be informed so that they can comply with these arrangements, and the second dwelling will NOT be sold. Mr. Feinstein will supply the name of the State uncouple counselor as well as continue to work toward standard uncoupling."

Judge Abraham gave her gavel a very firm and final slam.

Gwen just stared at her, face etched with horror, as the judge listed the details of her ruling. Judge Abraham couldn't be serious. Follow the rules as set by the State? No, most espouse proceedings were fast-tracked these days due to both the change to no-fault espouse laws and that couples espousing now reached close to 50 percent. Judge Abraham seemed to be stuck in the 1950s! The only reason Judge Abraham had done this was simple:

She hated Gwen.

The moment the judge finished, Gwen leapt to her feet. "Your Honor, I object! I object on the grounds that this is an unnecessary waste of time and resources. Even Mr. Feinstein agrees that this is unnecessary considering that New York is now a no-fault espouse state ..."

"Why even object, *Ms.* Stevens?" Judge Abraham said in a voice that was more of an inhuman growl than anything. She pretended to stretch and yawn. "Overruled."

Judge Abraham slammed the gavel down again to indicate that they were done, but Gwen continued to stare, the rage inside her reaching a boiling point. The Healys, beside her, whispered to one another, and then Sara tried to ask Gwen a question, but Gwen wasn't listening.

"All rise," the bailiff called out, and everyone stood.

Judge Abraham stood and peered down at Gwen. She clearly got off on being above her, up there, wielding her power like some mighty despot. "Is there something else, *Ms.* Stevens?"

Gwen called out, as loudly as she could, "Yes, my name is *Mrs. Stevens.*"

The judge flashed her an angry look before sweeping out of the room, her long dark robe like the black plumage of a buzzard following behind her. Gwen felt a flash of victory, but it only lasted a second because she knew now that she had to explain to her clients what just happened, even though Gwen wasn't sure if she knew herself.

Sara and Tom stared at one another, baffled. "I take it," Tom said softly as Gwen sat down in her chair and faced the couple head-on, "that this didn't go as planned?"

"Okay, this doesn't feel like a very good start?" Sara said, gripping her husband's hand for dear life while staring at Gwen. "I thought you said this was standard procedure and the judge would ease the rules because our case was straightforward; that the laws had changed to make getting espoused easier?"

Gwen swallowed. In the la-la land she'd been living in, where Judge Abraham was an adult and not a vindictive wench who insisted on treating them like felons, yes, that was how it should've gone.

Now ... who knew? All bets were off.

"Well, I—"

"We'll really have to separate?" Sara wailed.

"And I thought the children would be spared the school counseling? And what is the point of sending us to uncouple counseling, too?" Tom pointed out.

"Yes, yes," Gwen said softly but confidently. "But not every judge is so understanding of people wanting to espouse. Some are sticklers to what they can impose according to the law."

"Well ... can we get another judge to—"

Gwen was already shaking her head. "It doesn't work that way."

The Healys began to pepper Gwen with more and more questions. "Are we going to have to live apart for a full six months? Does this mean it will take longer? Is it possible that we can do everything right and still not be granted the espouse decree?"

The answers, Gwen knew, were yes, yes, and yes—answers she knew her clients wouldn't like, and she couldn't bring herself to tell them.

But with Carly Abraham as the judge overseeing this case, the worst was almost a definite.

Gwen tried to pull herself together in order to give her clients a pep talk when they needed it most. But how could she tell them that the only way they'd failed was by choosing her to represent them?

This was her fault.

Gwen opened her mouth to speak and looked up to see Kadir approaching, giving her a rueful look. Gwen took a few steps from her clients so she could speak frankly to Kadir. He shrugged. "Hey. Sorry, seems you got the judge on a bad day," he said quietly.

Gwen stared at him, incredulous. *Doesn't he remember who the judge is? And who we have in common?* "Or just a regular day," she muttered.

"Well, she's had to take on a lot more cases with Judge Gardner out."

Was Kadir defending her? Gwen didn't have time for this. She couldn't imagine how he worked day in, day out, with such a horrible woman. Kadir was a friendly person whom everyone liked and yet she'd heard stories from Riya about how Carly Abraham was always finding fault with him. Why he would defend her was beyond Gwen. "Right, I'm sure that's it," she muttered, rolling her eyes.

Kadir gave Gwen a *yeah, that's how the judge works* look, turned, and proceeded to go back to the judge's chambers while Gwen walked back to her clients, trying to think of the best way to break the bad news. Now more than ever, they needed a cheerleader, someone to tell them all was not lost.

Instead, Gwen saw Robert Feinstein, who had walked over and was standing right in front of her clients, looking through his iPhone. "Okay, Gwen, let me find the number of the uncouple counselor. Her name is Dr. Teresa Reed. She is good at handling couples who believe they want to espouse. Also, let's set up that appointment to make sure we don't get behind on the uncoupling process. I'm good Wednesday—"

"Hey," Gwen snapped. "Give us a break. We just got this news. Before we go and upend anyone's life, can we please give them a chance to breathe? Send me the number for Dr. Reed. I will forward it to my clients. And then let the Healys check their calendars for a date to meet you."

Robert held up his hands in surrender. He backed up, grabbed his briefcase off the table, and proceeded up the center aisle. "I'll text you the number and wait for the Healys to call me. You have my number," he said, not bothering to look back at them as he walked out of the courtroom.

Finally, they were alone in the courtroom. Gwen took a few deep breaths, trying to get her thoughts in order. *Lord, did I really yell at Judge Abraham "My name is Mrs. Stevens?" Why don't I just go ahead and tell the Healys they will never be espoused?*

Gwen turned to the Healys.

"Okay. Yes. This was a major setback. But it's not the end of the world. There are things we can do," she said, managing a smile. "I want you to go home, reset yourselves into understanding this will take a little longer, and try not to worry too much. Things will work out in the end."

That was something Dennis always said to her. *Things will work out in the end. If they haven't worked out, it's not the end.*

Both Healys nodded doubtfully at her as they pulled on their coats. She escorted them to the doors of the courtroom, hands on their shoulders, speaking calming words that were as much for her as they were for them.

When Gwen was alone in the courtroom, she rushed back to the table to find her phone. She found Kadir's number and jabbed in a text to him. *Can you let me know Abraham's schedule for tomorrow?*

She couldn't let the judge turn this case into any more of a clown show than it already was. Gwen needed to talk with the Wicked Witch of the Bench one-on-one.

CHAPTER 15

A Green Thumb

RIYA SHRUGGED OFF HER SWEATER since it was such a sunny and unseasonably warm November day. She threw open all the windows and helped Dennis outside to the garden to "shake the dust off," as she liked to say. The poor man hadn't been outdoors unless he was being shuttled to and from doctor's appointments. Riya believed a dose of fresh air would do Dennis's body good.

And it was a lovely garden, complete with a babbling brook, trellises, stone pathways, and heaps of mature greenery, with some still surviving flowers. It looked like a page out of Riya's favorite children's book, *The Secret Garden,* which she and Anaya had read at least a dozen times together. One couldn't help but be at peace out here.

Dennis sat on a cushioned glider surrounded by pillows, looking a little like a pampered prince. Riya had been able to find one of Gwen's pink sun visors in the hall closet, so she'd put that on him and wrapped him in a blanket to keep him from getting chilled.

"There now," Riya said, sitting beside him in an Adirondack chair on the deck overlooking their mature gardens. "Your garden is looking lovely these days."

Dennis harrumphed. Riya knew Dennis had been a meticulous gardener when he'd been well. When he became sick, Gwen had tried to keep up but then admitted to Riya that she had a black thumb. Gwen hired someone to take care of the lawn, bushes, and flowers, but it wasn't the same. Dennis had poured his heart and soul into this backyard, and it had shown. As he withered, so, too, did his beautiful garden.

Dennis frowned. "It needs tending to."

"Oh, it's pretty," Riya argued. "Just enjoy it. In another few months, there'll be piles of snow out here."

Riya poured him a cup of tea and handed it to him, noting the crease in his forehead. She could see him sizing up the garden with what he'd like to do to it. "We had the biggest strawberries over there once," Dennis murmured, pointing at one of the trellises. "Gwen loves strawberries."

"Does she?" Riya mused. "You know, you could tell her how to grow them?"

There was laughter in his eyes. "She kills just about every living plant she comes in contact with."

Riya slapped his arm lightly. "That's a terrible thing to say!"

"Oh, Gwen would be the first to say that it's true. She doesn't have the power to nurture much of anything ... except for Terrell. And me. No, with me, I'd say she is the one keeping me alive."

Riya smiled at him. "Did you two meet in court?"

Dennis nodded, looking up at the clouds racing fast across the whispery blue sky. "Yes. She was new to the court, maybe a few months. I kept seeing her in the hallways, wanting to talk to her, but she was always rushing from here to there. You know, typical Gwen. Never stops to smell the roses."

Riya nodded with understanding.

"One day, she was rushing into court, bumped into someone, and her briefcase fell to the ground, spilling open. I leaned down to help her and made my move."

Riya grinned, imagining the frail man in front of her during happier times. "And the rest is history?"

"Oh, no." He laughed. "I asked her out for coffee, and she turned me down flat. She told me to get away from her, that she was perfectly able to clean up her own messes. And then she called me a creep and sped away."

Riya raised an eyebrow. "She actually called you a creep?"

Dennis raised his hand in oath and crossed his heart. "Turned out she thought I was still married even though I'd uncoupled from Carly about five months prior. I started going to watch her when the court was in session, and whenever I could catch up to her, I'd ask her out. She kept saying no."

"Wow. Really? What was her excuse?"

"Oh, there was a different one every time. She had to feed her cat, or wash her hair, or meet a friend. But I didn't give up. And then a few months later, when I was in front of the courtroom, pleading an espouse case, I looked up, and who should I see in the back of the courtroom?"

Riya's mouth opened in surprise. Of course, Gwen would do things on her terms. "So, Gwen came to watch you?" When Dennis nodded, she said, "And then did she go out for coffee with you?"

"Nope. Our first date was in the rotunda of the courtroom. We shared a bag of potato chips during recess, and the entire time she peppered me with questions about my past."

"Are you serious?"

Dennis shrugged. "She is a suspicious thing, my Gwen."

"Of you?" Riya had been Dennis's home-care nurse for some time, and she'd never met a person who reminded her more of an overstuffed teddy bear. "Why?"

"Because she thought there had to be something wrong with me. She didn't understand how someone who fought so hard for the espouse rights of others could uncouple from his own wife."

"And why did you? Would you have uncoupled if it wasn't the law?"

The breeze was picking up. Dennis pulled the blanket over his shoulders. "I'll tell you the same thing I told her. Sometimes people marry and they move together. In the case of Carly and me, we moved apart. We fought all the time, we fell out of love and wanted to live different lives. When the time came to uncouple, neither of us fought it. It was the right thing to do. It seemed natural."

A cloud sailed over the sun, making it colder. "I guess we should go inside," Riya suggested.

Dennis gathered himself up and rose slowly to his feet. Grabbing onto her upper arm for support, he said to her, "I don't regret it. It was the right decision because it led me to Gwen and my son."

Riya smiled, but inside, she had to wonder. Would she and Kadir drift apart and uncouple so easily? It seemed impossible. In fact, her heart already felt heavy with regret even though the final uncoupling documents hadn't yet been signed.

CHAPTER 16

Lunch Time

THE CRISPNESS IN THE AIR didn't stop all the kids from eating outside in the courtyard at Oldfield Middle School. Avery was late because Ms. Kim had cornered her in the hall, asking her once again about her *feelings*, so by the time she got out of the line with her lunch of a misshapen hamburger and soggy french fries, all the spots with her usual friends were taken. Scarlet hadn't even saved her a seat. *The wench*, thought Avery, using one of her SAT words.

Maybe they were all shunning her because of the E-word.

No, that was ridiculous. That wasn't her fault.

Avery scanned for an empty place to sit, certain that once they saw her standing alone, they'd beckon her over and make room.

She saw Anaya sitting alone at a table. Avery veered over to her former bestie, walking slowly in case her friends would notice and invite Avery to sit with them.

They didn't. She heard Scarlet blabbing about some *a-mahzing* thing that happened to her in study hall, to which everyone appeared to be raptly listening.

Sighing, Avery made it to the picnic table and noisily dropped her tray with dramatic effect. Anaya, nose buried in a book, didn't even look up. *What, am I invisible?*

"Can I sit here?" Avery asked.

Anaya startled. "What?" She moved her book away and nibbled absently on a sandwich as her eyes drifted back to the page. "Yeah. Sure."

"Must be a good book," Avery said.

Anaya flipped the cover to her. *The Great Gatsby.*

Wait. Wasn't that a schoolbook? "Good" and "Required Reading" simply didn't go together in the same sentence.

Avery opened her burger and looked at the gray thing they passed off as meat between the buns. It made her stomach twist.

Just then, a laugh erupted from the table where her friends were sitting. Avery glanced at them, frowning. *Really?*

"So, what's new?" she asked Anaya nonchalantly, desperate by now for *some* kind of human interaction.

Anaya shrugged. "Same old thing." She looked back at her book and then up at Avery. "Why are you here?"

Avery blinked. "What?"

Anaya hooked a thumb toward Avery's friends. "You usually sit with them. What, didn't they have a seat for you?"

Avery sighed, wondering if she was this transparent to everyone or just the people who knew her super-well, like Anaya. "Why? Can't I sit with you? I mean, we're friends, right?"

Anaya eyed her warily. "Yes, I guess so. But you usually find more interesting company during lunch period. Isn't James around?"

She blushed. "What?" *Oh, God.* Yes, she liked James. A lot. But was it so obvious to everyone? *Am I going overboard? Giggling too loud? Mooning obnoxiously, the way a lot of girls seem to do around James?* "What are you talking about? He and I have been friends for, like, forever. Like you and me."

Anaya raised an eyebrow. "Believe me, it is *nothing* like you and me."

"I have no clue what you're talking about." Avery crossed her arms, suddenly feeling chilly despite wearing a Lululemon yoga jacket. Over at the other table, laughter erupted again. It sounded like the laugh track on some lame sitcom.

Avery dug her fingernails into her thighs as Anaya went back to her book.

"So, you're seriously just going to ignore me?" Avery reached over and grabbed the book out of Anaya's hands. Anaya tried to snatch it back, but she moved too slowly.

Anaya took a breath and sighed, "Come on. Just give it back."

Frowning, Avery returned the book to her. The jerks she used to call her friends were now passing around someone's phone and laughing at whatever … probably an Instagram post of Scarlet and Rob … and not a single one of them noticing her. She felt tears prick her eyes. *Why is everything falling apart?*

"Are you okay?"

Avery swiped at her cheek as she realized that Anaya had closed her book and was now staring at her, concerned. Anaya was like that, the nurturer, like her own mom. Always concerned about everyone. Sometimes Avery felt like that was all their friendship ever was—Anaya was always giving her things, and Avery was always taking. But Anaya never seemed to mind.

The way Anaya stared at her had always made her want to pour her heart out. Avery threw a napkin over the travesty that was trying to pass itself off as a burger, slumped over the table, and fed a too-salty fry into her mouth. "My parents. Espousing. It sucks."

Anaya's eyes widened. "Oh."

This would be the time when Anaya would offer her a little *Anaya Wisdom*. Don't worry about things that don't worry about you. Life gets better. Make lemons out of lemonade.

But she didn't. Anaya's eyes trailed to the surface of the picnic table, and she let out a big sigh.

It was in the silence that Avery suddenly realized that Anaya's parents were probably approaching their uncoupling date.

"So, when are your parents uncoupling? Must be coming up soon? You are so lucky to have such great parents who don't think only of themselves but of you, too."

Anaya just shrugged her shoulders, grabbed her half-eaten sandwich, and stuffed it into a paper bag. Avery was confused. *What did I say? Doesn't anyone want to hang out with me?*

"Hey, guys."

Avery looked up, and her mouth nearly fell to the floor.

James was striding toward them, his eyes squinting and hair blowing romantically in the breeze. He looked like a young Tom Cruise from *Top Gun*, she thought, the movie she had watched with her mom last weekend. She could feel goosebumps popping up everywhere underneath her thick jacket. "Hi," she squeaked.

Then Avery looked at Anaya, who was studying her like, *I told you so,* and Avery tried to force herself to play it as cool as possible. She'd leave. That was it. Just get up and walk away.

But something had her rooted to the spot.

Before Avery could overcome that feeling, Anaya swung her legs out from under the table and started to leave first. "See you guys later," she called over her shoulder.

James started to sit down next to Avery, but an image of herself giggling too loudly filled her head. She sprang up. "I've got to go."

"You do?" he said, surprised. "Are you okay?"

Avery looked around nervously. Then her eyes met his, and once again, she felt the desire to stay in that spot and never leave. "Yes ... I mean ... you know. It's a parent thing."

James let out a laugh. "I saw your parents in Starbucks the other day. I get it."

Avery's stomach sank. "Did they seem sickeningly in love? Did they behave that way in public?"

He nodded. "Sorry."

Avery lowered her head and blushed. "How freakishly embarrassing." She gnawed on her lower lip. "And of course, I'll be freakish by association."

James's brow wrinkled. "What are you talking about? You? You're not even close to being a freak."

She was surprised at his saying that. "Really? You don't think it's weird?"

He shook his head and dug his hands into the pockets of his jeans. "Maybe it's no big deal. It's happening more and more now. And think about it. You're going to save a lot of time not having to get your butt shuttled between parents. That's got to be worth something."

Avery wasn't sure if it was what James was saying or the way he was saying it in that soothing, deep voice he got only a year ago. She managed a half-smile. "You think?"

James nodded. "Definitely."

Avery smiled while laughter roared over at the other table. She looked over to see Scarlet whispering something in Rob's ear. He was straddling the seat facing her, and they looked awfully cozy. "Why aren't you sitting with them?" Avery asked James.

James hitched a shoulder and tossed his face back to the sky. "Because I came over to sit with you, silly."

It was early November and feeling chilly, but that didn't make a difference. Avery was melting like an ice cube on a hot summer day.

CHAPTER 17

Stuck in the Middle

CARLY ABRAHAM needed a cigarette.

Didn't matter that she had quit twenty years ago after doctors had found her blood pressure to be too high, which scared the hell out of her. Right now, she was craving one.

"Kadir, really," she said, slumping behind her desk in her chambers. "Give me a break."

Kadir stopped talking at once and shoved his hands into his pockets. He took a breath, and she knew he wasn't done yet.

Judge Abraham held up a finger before he could get the next syllable out. "Stop. No. The answer is no." When he gave her a silent, pleading look, she shook her head. "You're very cute, which is why I keep you around. But you're damned stubborn, and you don't know when to stop."

Kadir sighed. The judge knew he hated being called cute, handsome, pretty boy, all the nicknames she had for him ... which was why she persisted with them. He said, "Look. I really do believe you should think about granting Mrs. Stevens an audience to air her concerns."

"What will it matter?" she shot back, crossing her arms. "I've already explained what *Ms.* Stevens should do. I'm not changing my mind. As far as I'm concerned, the matter's over. I'm not meeting with her. I've denied the request, and that's that."

"You're going to have to have discovery anyway, right?" Kadir said. "Maybe then that will help her see your point of view."

The phone buzzed in his pocket, and Kadir fished it out. He apologized, turned it to silent, and waited for her response. Judge Abraham usually hated the distraction of cell phones, but she seemed interested in who was calling him. "Who's that?"

He shook his head dismissively. "No one. My wife. Now—"

"Answer it, my boy," she stated, challenging the poor man. Kadir looked at her, bewildered. The judge quickly demanded, "Now. Answer it."

On any ordinary day, she would've snatched the phone from his hands and admonished him while complaining about how "people today can't disconnect for five minutes!"

"You serious?" said Kadir, still not too sure. *Is this a trick?*

"Yep." She laced her hands in front of her and waited patiently.

Kadir studied the judge curiously as he brought the phone to his ear. Before he could utter a stilted hello, Riya started babbling a mile a minute. She finally ended with, "What did you do?"

"Sorry, Riya," he said, grated by her tone. She was clearly still in a mood. "Could you back up?"

Riya let out an annoyed sigh. "I noticed that the uncoupling documents were still on the table at home. Weren't you going to mail them? Did you forget again?"

"Well, I—" he started. What had lit a fire under her? "You still need to sign them, and—"

"Signed. They just need your signature."

Kadir tightened his hand on the receiver. She had? "I didn't realize—"

"There will be a late fee if we don't light a fire under it. We do have to have a conversation with Anaya, too. Kadir, I know she will be fine, it's natural, but she said some strange things the other night. I don't know where her head is."

Kadir nodded. "Yeah. I agree, she certainly wasn't herself," he said, his eyes on the judge, who followed his conversation closely. Too closely. He worried he was saying something wrong. Riya tried to continue, but Kadir could no longer endure the glare of the judge, so he quickly tried to end the conversation with a change in subject. "Yeah. I'll pick up Anaya and a gallon of milk on the way home. Look, the judge just walked in, and I've got to go." He prepared to put his phone away.

"How's he doing?" Judge Abraham suddenly interrupted.

He looked up quizzically at the judge and asked, "Who?"

"Dennis."

Dennis? This seemed a little out of left field. But, fine.

Riya sounded confused. "What milk? We are talking about Anaya?"

Kadir broke into her stream of consciousness. "How's Dennis today? Yeah. Dennis." He nodded as Riya answered him. "Oh. Good." Kadir pulled away from the phone and said to the judge, "All good."

The judge acknowledged the response with a curt nod, and then, as Riya tried to continue her conversation about Anaya, the judge said, "Kadir. Are you going to stay on that phone all blessed day?"

"No. No ma'am," he said, flustered, accidentally speaking into the phone instead of to the judge. He said to Riya, "I've got to go," ending the call swiftly, without waiting for a response from his wife.

The judge picked up her pen and said, "Get a date on the schedule for a meeting in the courtroom with Stevens and Feinstein. Don't let it interfere with tennis. Got it?"

He thumbed a note into his phone. "For?"

"Discovery, hearing of facts, and legal motions regarding the requests for the Healys. Let's get this done."

CHAPTER 18

Following the Rules

A VERY TENSE KADIR PASSUD scratched his fingernails over his palms as he entered the courtroom the following week.

He'd thought he'd been through a war with Riya over the past few days regarding their pending uncoupling.

But this truly felt like D-Day.

As Kadir strode to the front of the court and laid the file on Judge Abraham's desk, he looked around. Everyone looked slightly afraid, like soldiers about to enter their first battle, with no idea whether they'd leave alive. The tension was so thick even Kadir could barely breathe, and he wasn't even pleading this case. Pulling on the collar of his starched white shirt, he wondered why it felt like a thousand degrees inside the room.

He looked at Gwen, who was quietly speaking with the Healys. He wanted to mouth good luck to her, but she needed more than that.

She needed a miracle.

The bailiff bellowed, "All rise," and as they all stood, the judge ambled in and stopped at the bench, not looking up at anyone. She waved at everyone to sit as she slumped into her chair, obviously in another one of her wonderful moods.

"All right, let's get this show on the road," the judge grumbled.

Robert Feinstein stood. "Your Honor, I—"

She held up a hand and did not even look at him. "Stop. Not you. I seriously want to hear from anyone *but* you right now. I would rather hear a root canal drill than your whiny voice."

Robert stopped and swallowed, a smile of amusement appearing on his face. It was like he enjoyed the punishment. Gwen imagined Judge Abraham breaking out a paddle on his backside and him screaming out, *Thank you, ma'am, may I have another?*

"Now," Judge Abraham said. "This is a discovery hearing regarding the Healy espouse case. I really don't know what there is left for us to discover. I believe I've made myself clear to you, *Ms.* Stevens?"

The judge did a number on drawing out the *Ms.*, letting it hiss off her tongue while giving Gwen a superior glance.

Gwen stood. "You've made yourself clear, but I don't think you're being fair."

The judge straightened her robe, staring at the ceiling, and rolled her eyes before addressing Gwen. "I did everything allowable by law. What's your problem?"

Gwen pressed her lips together defiantly. "My problem? With all due respect, Your Honor, I don't think I'm the one with the problem. I didn't request anything that is not allowable by law, especially now that New York is a no-fault espouse state. These people want to stay together. It will be difficult enough settling all the tax issues, dealing with their children's well-being, as well as all the other logistics. You can make a difference between a long, drawn-out, expensive, emotional nightmare for them or a constructive ending to this uncoupling, resulting in the Healys becoming espoused. I urge you to be merciful here."

When Gwen was done, the whole room went quiet. About thirty seconds went by without a single word from the judge. To Kadir, it felt like an eternity. He knew in his gut that when the judge responded, it was not going to go well. The judge laced her hands together and leaned forward as if she was about to impart a thoughtful reply.

Instead, she simply opened her mouth and let out an ear-splitting honk of a, "HA!"

Gwen let out the breath she'd been holding and frowned at the judge.

"Merciful?" the judge began, shaking her head. "You come in here and clog up my courtroom with this drivel, and you want mercy? There is a law that requires people to uncouple. It is on the books because it works. It is not natural for two people to spend their lives together. Espousing is not natural. Because it is not natural, the State must step in to make sure people understand the seriousness of not uncoupling. So, I say that the Healys need this trial separation. They might even learn that it's what's best for them. This is the law."

Gwen slammed her palms down on the table in front of her. "It's cruel, is what it is! Who are you to decide what reasons they want to stay together? Maybe it's for the kids. Maybe it's for financial reasons. Maybe—and hold onto your hat for this one—maybe they just still love each other! It can happen! People do stay in love longer than fifteen years!"

The judge leaned forward, studying the woman in front of her. Gwen was shaking, she was so angry, but she also looked strangely fragile, too, like a stiff wind would blow her over. "Love? So, tell me. Do you really think Dennis would still be with you if you had been his first wife? Are you telling me the two of you would've fought to be espoused?"

Gwen looked at the judge, completely speechless. She was arguing for the Healys. Not for Dennis. This was completely uncalled-for. She opened her mouth to tell the judge that, but she knew she'd probably get held in contempt.

The judge saw the hesitation and went in for the kill. "What if our roles had been reversed? What if you were married to Dennis first? He would have uncoupled from you, and I would now be married to him for all these years. Have you ever thought of that?"

Gwen stood there, shaking, pressing her hands into the table to keep from slumping to her chair. She dropped her gaze to the table and shook her head. Yes, she had thought about all of that. More than was healthy, probably. She often wondered if Dennis had loved Carly as much as he loved her.

After a moment's silence, Gwen settled into her seat. So that was it. This wasn't about discovery. This was about finding another way to skewer her for being Dennis's second wife. The one he picked after he uncoupled from Judge Abraham.

"The Healys are to have a six-month trial separation. Their children will attend counseling and follow the uncoupled children's schedule of visitation. Sara and Thomas Healy will attend uncouple counseling with Dr. Teresa Reed. I believe Mr. Feinstein has already supplied them her number?" and then Judge Abraham finished with, "I will see you in the courtroom in months four and six to check in to see how things are going."

Robert Feinstein stood. "I'm fine with discovery for months four and six to be between Ms. Stevens and myself since it will just be proof of documents and following procedure."

Judge Abraham gave him a sour look. "Denied. I will make sure all the documents, including the financial affidavits, are in order, Mr. Feinstein. Do not tell me what you are FINE with in my courtroom."

She banged her gavel and stood up. "I'm done here. You're excused, *Ms.* Stevens."

Vanessa squeaked out, "All rise," as the judge stood to leave the bench.

Gwen felt the vomit gurgling in the back of her throat as she rose, nodding. The judge watched her hurry out of the courtroom with her clients, who, shell-shocked, were quietly murmuring to each other about the meaning of the ruling as they followed Gwen.

Kadir followed the Healys with his eyes, wishing Judge Gardner had not taken sick, for Gwen's sake. Then he looked down at the ground, pulling on his collar. It absolutely was too damn hot in here.

Judge Abraham looked at him and shrugged. "So. What time is the next case? Do you have time to run down to Starbucks to get me a latte?"

CHAPTER 19

The Separation—Month One

SARA RAN HER HANDS over her tired face and looked out at the sea of boxes in front of her.

As much as she loved Tom, she had to admit he was a bit of a slob. Tom kept everything. The deer horns from the buck he'd killed hunting with his dad when he was thirteen? A beer mug from college with the Hofstra College insignia peeling off? A hideous railroad spike sculpture he'd bought ... who knows where? And what the heck was with this beer can lamp?

Tom wrangled with a garbage sack, trying to wrestle it out onto the curb. "Why do I need that? Toss it," he said, glancing at her.

Sara looked down into her hands at a copy of *The Elements of Style* that she'd gotten in college. "Because it's an important guide for—"

"We have two other copies in better shape," he said. "You might need yours, but I don't need one where I'm going. Trust me. That one's missing a cover. Just toss it."

Sara threw it over to him, and Tom tossed it in the bag. Funny how the separation had morphed into an opportunity to scour the house in a way that they had not done in … thirteen years? She'd found ancient Cheerios in the sofa from when Sam was a toddler. Gross!

But now she was tired. Tom had his suitcases in the foyer, and he'd packed several boxes of belongings into a U-Haul. He was good to go. But all he'd been doing for the past half-hour was delaying.

"Now remember, you need to make sure the thermostat is under sixty-five at night or else we're going to be paying a boatload on heating," he said. "Garbage night is Tuesday, recycling Wednesday, and garbage again on Friday. Do you need me to write any of this down for you?"

Sara rolled her eyes. "No. Believe it or not, I'm not just a house sitter. I have been living here right along with you, Tom."

He frowned at her. "Right. Right. I'm sorry. Just … this is all so weird."

Sara admitted it was. But she felt a little excited about the idea. It all started the moment they talked about splitting checking accounts. It suddenly occurred to her what that meant. Those $250 shoes she'd been eyeing at Macy's? They could be hers, without the bat of an eyelash, without having to endure the disappointed look and the, "Well, if they mean that much to you" Tom would give her. Sara had joined a new fitness gym in town to get back into exercising. She had also pitched for additional freelance writing jobs for *The New Yorker*, and they wanted to see her, which meant Sara would have to make an appointment for a haircut and color. As Sara was cleaning out the house, she eviscerated her closet, too. What was with all the mom jeans and cardigans?

But it wasn't just that. No longer would she have Tom looking over her shoulder for every household decision. No longer would she have to ask him for his opinion. ... Now, the buck stopped with her.

The thought was scary at first but now sounded a little ... thrilling.

Sara just wanted him to go already. She wanted the prosecutor to split those accounts. She imagined herself walking downtown in those sexy little pumps.

Avery also must have sensed it. Sara knew the kids were on the stairs listening to them bicker over every last thing. She only realized how annoyed Avery was when her daughter called down, "Can you put a lid on it, people! I've got homework!"

Avery, who hadn't willingly done homework in, well ... ever.

Finally, Tom got all his belongings together, shoved the screen door open, and then headed to his car. Sara noticed a box Tom had left behind and grabbed it while following him out, so he wouldn't have to come back in. "Say goodbye to Dad!" she called up to the kids.

The kids let out an unenthusiastic goodbye. Tom frowned. "Nice to see they're going to miss me."

Sara sighed. "It's not like it's so-long forever."

Tom pushed his suitcases into the back of his Range Rover. "Right. I'll see them every night for dinner. And of course, over the weekends."

Sara clenched her teeth. "About that. I know we said separation be damned. No one could stop us from seeing each other every day. But maybe we should try to go by the parenting schedule that the court has set up for us? So that this can be done right?"

Tom's eyes grew big. "But ..."

"I'm just worried. If we don't go by the rules, it could jeopardize our espouse. And I don't want to take that chance."

"Ah." Tom hadn't thought about that.

Sara saw the opening and jumped in. "That judge doesn't seem to like us much. Maybe if we put in an effort, she and the prosecutor will take pity on us, and things will go better in court."

Tom nodded, relieved. "Yeah. You know, you're right. That makes sense. It'll be tough but worth it in the end."

He went over to the car and got inside. He started it, pulled away, and Sara watched him slowly go down the driveway. She let out a breath, put her hands in her back pockets, and turned to go back into the house.

Suddenly, Tom came to a screeching stop at the end of the driveway. Sara, startled, turned around. He rolled down the window and waved to her. She approached him. "Forget something?"

"The most important thing," he said with a grin. "I forgot to give you a goodbye kiss."

"Oh, right."

Sara leaned in, grabbed his head with her hands, put her lips on his, stuck her tongue in his mouth, and French kissed him. Sara and Tom hadn't done that in quite a while, and it was fun! Sara thought, *Maybe this separation would be good?* She would miss Tom.

Sara waved to him as he finally pulled out of sight, then turned to look back at the house. What was this feeling bubbling in her chest? Excitement? Fear? Here she was, alone in her home for the first time in fifteen years. She could watch her own movies on television, leave her clothes on the floor, cook something Tom would have hated for dinner ... it didn't matter.

Sara had to admit this was going to be an adventure.

It won't be for long, though, she told herself, forcing her heart to stop leaping in her chest. *When I get into bed tonight, I bet I'll feel lonely. And then it will just get worse from there.*

CHAPTER 20

Some Good News

GWEN SAT IN THE DOCTOR'S OFFICE, her son Terrell's hand in hers as she studied his strong profile. Handsome and tall, he had his father's nose and strong jaw.

She'd spent a lot of time thinking of the things Carly Abraham had said about what if the roles were reversed and whether Dennis would've loved her enough to want to espouse. But when she looked at Terrell, all of that seemed silly. She had him. And together, she and Dennis had raised an amazing young man. He was the best thing that had come from their marriage, which was all that mattered.

Terrell gave her a nudge and said, "Ma. Calm down. It'll be okay. Whatever it is, we'll get through it."

Terrell didn't realize that Dennis's health hadn't been what was making her brow knit. But the second Terrell reminded her, she stroked his hand, thankful that he'd made the trip down from Boston to be with her when she needed him most. Dennis, on her other side, was looking better today. Stronger. When Gwen looked at him this way, wearing his Irish cap, blue jeans, and a tailored shirt, he almost looked like the old Dennis before cancer.

Dr. Patel, one of Long Island's top oncologists, had a very curt demeanor. Gwen knew not to expect a lot of flowery language—he'd give it to them straight and fast, the way you would rip off a Band-Aid. When the doctor walked in, he shook each of their hands warmly, then sat down at his desk and opened the file.

"I'm encouraged," Dr. Patel said, causing Gwen to exhale in relief, even before he finished his report. "The cancer has shrunk significantly. In fact, it is barely noticeable. No more chemo. Next step is radiation and the continuation of immunotherapy."

Terrell squeezed her hand. Gwen said, "Oh, thank—"

"It's still very early, Mrs. Stevens. So please don't think we're out of the woods yet. This was a clinical trial, but in my eyes, a successful one."

Gwen looked over at Dennis, who was grinning from ear to ear. "I might not be out of the woods, but I can see the path through the clearing, Doc!"

Dennis had an energy to him Gwen hadn't seen in months. He looked about ready to do a jig. The doctor held out his hands to slow him down. "Dennis, you still need to get your strength back. That's what the name of the game is right now. So, no stress. And that means no work. At least until we have a few good months behind us."

"Of course, I always do what the doctor orders," he quipped, winking at Gwen.

They were all smiles as they made it to the parking garage. Terrell had taken them in his Hyundai, so Dennis climbed up front, and Gwen climbed into the back, sitting on the middle bump so she didn't miss looking at her men.

"I feel like a burger and fries at Meehan's," Dennis said. "To celebrate."

"Hold on, hold on. What happened to doing what the doctor ordered? You still need to stick to your diet," Gwen said to her husband.

"Aw, Ma," Terrell said, pulling out of the space. "Burger and fries for the old guy? He's been living on beans and sprouts for the past six months."

"No, he hasn't!" Gwen said, smacking her son but laughing just the same. "Geez, you make me feel like Riya and I have been drill sergeants."

Dennis smiled at her. "Well, whatever you've been doing, I can't complain. It's working."

Gwen studied her husband, feeling truly happy for the first time in ... how long had it been? Everything was so positive. *More of this, and I won't have to worry about Dennis. We could go back to living our lives again. What would that be like?* Could she consider going back to corporate law and stop being an espouse lawyer?

Gwen frowned when she remembered the last time she was in the courtroom with Judge Abraham. What a fiasco that had been. *That intolerable woman!* She had some nerve.

"You thinking of that case with the Healys again?" Dennis quizzed her.

She didn't want to talk about it. "No, I'm ..." she stopped. "How did you know that?"

"Because you always get that tiny little crinkle between your eyes, and your hands form into fists." Dennis reached his arm between the console and took her hand. Gwen relaxed her fists and held his hand.

She sighed. "Yes. Well, I'm still upset with the ruling."

Terrell raised an eyebrow. "What case?"

Dennis said, "Your mother happens to be bringing an espouse case in front of Carly Abraham."

Terrell winced. He knew all about the judge from hearing her name mentioned over the years. Though Gwen and Dennis tried to keep his ex-wife out of their current relationship, a strong personality like Carly's always managed to creep in. "Yikes."

"It's not my first time arguing a case in front of her," Gwen said. "Though I can't say the other two were joyous occasions either. I feel like she's getting more witchy in her old age."

Their son pulled in front of Meehan's as Dennis released her hand. "I'm sure it'll go fine, Sport."

They went inside and got Dennis exactly what he wanted—a medium-rare burger with fries, and for dessert, a vanilla ice cream with rainbow sprinkles. After all, this was a celebration.

When they arrived home, Gwen steered him to his downstairs room, but he shook his head. "What if I stay with you tonight?"

Gwen looked up, surprised, to see him winking at her.

She smiled. "Well, I suppose that would be fine."

They went upstairs, changed into their pajamas, and got into bed together. It felt nice to have her husband's warm body against hers. Gwen had almost forgotten how nice. "What if uncoupling wasn't the law?" she asked him quietly as they lay in bed, cuddling together.

Dennis closed his eyes. She knew he'd heard that so many times over the years.

"Gwen," he said to her, stroking her arm. "I am going to tell you the same thing I've said for over twenty-five years. I love you. I love our son. I love our life together. Love is all that matters."

Gwen knew that too. But she couldn't help those small seeds of doubt that continued to find root within her mind. She couldn't imagine a life without him. What if she had met him first when they were both embroiled in their careers? Would they be living apart now, completely unaware of what forever could have been like? Would they have gone through the rest of their lives feeling as though they were missing something to make them complete?

Gwen decided not to think about it anymore that night. That night, Dennis was in bed with her. It felt so right.

CHAPTER 21

You're Late

RIYA HAD TO GET BACK to the Stevens's house to tend to Dennis. Anaya had forgotten her lunch—strange for her, but Anaya hadn't been acting quite right for weeks—so Riya had to deliver it to the school. She also had about a thousand other things going on at home that she hadn't had a chance to handle—the bills on the dining room table had piled up, needing to be dealt with, this morning.

But now, as Riya strode into the courthouse with the papers in hand, she had only one thing on her mind.

Riya pushed open the door to the office where she had been directed to find Kadir. He wasn't there. Frowning, she went into the courtroom and saw him in front of the bench, stacking up some files.

"I need to talk to you," she said, frowning at him. "NOW."

This was as angry as Riya had ever been. And she never spoke so angrily to Kadir in public. But this time, she had a good reason.

Kadir, surprised, hesitated. Noticing people entering the courtroom, he took her hand and guided her through the back room into Judge Abraham's chambers. "This isn't a good time," he said. "I have a case in twenty minutes."

"It's never a good time, is it?" she sighed. "When will it be a good time? When these are late?"

Riya lifted the uncoupling documents out of her bag and threw them on the judge's desk.

"Because news flash, Kadir: they are late. Now we're going to have to pay a seventy-five-dollar fee."

Kadir looked down at the papers, then scrubbed a hand over his face. "I'm sorry."

"Sorry? Well, what's the problem?"

Riya sat back against the edge of the desk, waiting for Kadir to explain. He pressed his lips together. Something obviously distressed him. She found herself waiting anxiously for his next words. Maybe he'd finally say he didn't want to go through with it after all. Leave it to Kadir to be last-minute with everything. Holding her breath, she leaned forward, staring at him with wide eyes, hoping to draw those thoughts out of him.

Just then, the door swung open, and Judge Abraham appeared. She scowled. "Oh, don't mind me. I'm just the owner of this particular office."

Kadir straightened. "I'm sorry. I thought you'd be in later."

"Well, I came in early to go over cases." She pointed to the door. "Shoo."

Kadir nodded. "Yes. Of course." Then he looked at Riya and scooped the papers into his hands. "I'll personally take the uncoupling documents to Town Hall and submit them right away. Then we won't have to pay the fee. Okay?"

Riya tried to urge him out of the office. She was sure there was something he'd wanted to say, but he'd been interrupted. Maybe if they could find a quiet place, they could discuss …

"What's wrong with you, Kadir? Being late like that?" Judge Abraham was studying them from behind her desk. She made a tut-tutting noise with her tongue. "That's so out of character. You need to get your act together. It's unfair to your wife and daughter."

"Well, I—"

"I'm surprised at you, really," Judge Abraham continued. "It's not like you didn't know it was coming up. You should have been more on top of it."

Riya watched her husband absorb the judge's words, not saying anything to defend himself. The more she spoke, the smaller he looked, and less like the man she'd married.

Kadir escorted Riya out of Judge Abraham's office.

When they went outside, Riya looked at her husband. She waited for him to continue what he'd been saying before the judge entered her chambers, but he didn't. He looked wounded. He was clutching onto the documents for dear life.

"Then you'll submit them today?" Riya prompted him.

"Yes. I will," Kadir said.

Then I guess that's it, Riya thought as she left him, wandering down the hallway without much more than a goodbye. *I guess that's how it all ends. Not with a whimper but with a 'who cares'?*

CHAPTER 22

James Has Problems Too!

JAMES BAUM SAT BACK on his bed in his father's house and looked at the text from Avery. *Hey. You're going to love Scarlet's new uncoupling gift from her father.*

He looked at the text and smiled. They'd been texting nonstop over the Christmas break. He knew he should probably do something to try to make it official, like boyfriend-girlfriend. He thought Avery liked him, but putting himself out there, letting her and possibly everyone else know how he felt?

For now, James would stick to texting her. What if he asked her out and ruined everything?

Let me guess. A new phone.

Avery texted back, *Nope. Try a freaking horse!*

He let out an ironic laugh. Everyone knew that once parents uncoupled, it was common for them to give gifts because they didn't see their kids all the time or were competing with one another. But leave it to Scarlet to weasel a horse from her father. *Seriously?*

Yes, she's been texting me pictures of him all day long. Save me!

James smiled, trying to think of a way to reply as his little sister, Cara, cartwheeled into the room, practicing her latest gymnastic routine. "You ready to leave, James?" she asked him. "Mom will be here any minute."

Annoyed, he pointed to the duffel bag at the end of his bed.

"Who're you texting?" she asked, leaning against the door jamb. "Oh. Let me guess. Avery."

Cara sing-songed the name. Not looking up from the screen, he reached for his pillow to throw at her. At the house he shared with his mom, there were lots of pillows. But this was his dad's house, and his dad was a minimalist. He only had the one he was leaning on.

Cara turned her back on him and wrapped her arms tightly around herself, doing the hugging, make-out thing, where she made a bunch of smooching noises and said, *Oh Avery, you're so beautiful.*

James lifted the corner of his mouth in a snarl and spotted one of his Nikes on the ground, quickly scooping it up and launching it at her. Cara shrieked and ducked, so it hit a spot in the hallway with a loud thunk. "What about you and Sam?" he called after her.

He cringed when he saw the brown mark on the white wall. Dad would kill him.

Michael Baum called up, "Hey! Cut it out, you two!"

Just then the doorbell rang. Mom.

He quickly texted Avery, *My mom's here to pick me up from Dad's. Brb.*

James grabbed his duffel bag and slid off the bed. Shoving his foot into a Nike, he lumbered into the hallway, noting his handiwork on the wall. He found his other shoe, and as he stepped into it, he saw Cara standing on the top of the staircase, silent, holding her Hello Kitty backpack. "What, loser?" he said, giving Cara a wet willy.

"Ew!" She whirled around and shushed him. "Shh. Listen!"

Wondering why his little sister was being such a dork, he listened. He heard his mom and dad talking in the foyer. Jessica was explaining how crazy things were, which was why they hadn't been able to make their normal Starbucks appointment. Michael told her not to worry, things like that happened all the time.

Their parents were getting along. Not only that, but they were laughing. Laughing like they enjoyed each other's company?

That was weird enough. The entire last year before they'd uncoupled, they'd spent most of the time fighting. When they'd finally uncoupled, it was a weight off everyone's chest. Sure, he had to get used to the usual new stuff happening in his parents' lives, like seeing Mom happy with her pediatrician boyfriend and Dad with a little blonde college co-ed from Hofstra who was probably only ten years older than James and kind of looked like a young version of Mom. But ... as everyone knew, the potential for four parents instead of two was a good thing and very normal.

Cara looked at James, a horrified expression on her face. "What are they doing?" she whispered.

"Chill," James said, listening. Cara was, as usual, overreacting. They were just being civil. Uncoupled parents had to be civil. It's not like they had their tongues down each other's throats or anything. The uncoupling had worked—they could now talk to one another like adults.

Just then, James heard his mother burst into hysterical,

schoolgirl-style laughter. Okay, he had to admit, that was suspicious. Had he ever heard her laugh like that?

The two of them crept down the narrow staircase, shoulder to shoulder, listening. "What about the kids?" Jessica was saying. Michael laughed in a low rumble. "They can stay here tonight." Jessica, then: "But won't that interfere with your work schedule?" Michael: "Oh, no, I can drop the kids at school before work. As long as that's okay with you?"

A sick feeling rooted itself in James's stomach. There was civil, and then there was nauseatingly bending over backward to accommodate each other ... which was something his parents never did. *Who are these people? Did aliens take over my parents' bodies?*

When they reached the bottom step, James looked over and saw his parents standing close to one another, goofy expressions on their faces. Had he ever seen them standing that close to each other? *What the hell is going on?*

Jessica noticed James and Cara. "Oh, hey kids," she said. Was he mistaken or was there a hint of embarrassment in her voice?

"Did you just say we're staying here tonight?" Cara asked, her face twisted like she was in physical pain.

Their dad came up to them and punched James on the shoulder. "Yeah. Hey. How 'bout you guys stay put tonight. Your mom and I are going to go out. No sense going to your mom's after we get back."

"Out? Where?" Cara blurted.

"Movies. Dinner," Michael said with a shrug. "We're grown adults. We can figure it out."

Michael looked at Jessica, who grinned at him as if he was the funniest comedian in the world.

"It's a school night, so remember, ten o'clock bedtime," Michael said.

What the ...? This was bad. Very bad. And just plain weird. They were successfully uncoupled and loving it. Right? "Okay," James said doubtfully, retreating upstairs.

Cara came into his room wanting to discuss it, like she discussed everything, with a lot of OMGs and hysterics. James couldn't deal with it. He pushed her out of his room, and as he locked the door, he heard his parents leaving, and his mother ... was she giggling?

Really, what was this? *The Twilight Zone?*

James understood Cara's need to share. He *had* to talk to someone about this.

He pulled out his phone and texted Avery: *You will never guess what just happened here.*

CHAPTER 23

Uncouple Counseling

DR. TERESA REED SAT at her small, mahogany, Victorian-style desk, reviewing the file of Sara and Tom Healy. Half her clients were couples trying to manage through the changes of uncoupled life. The other half were court-appointed, couples looking to espouse, and she was to determine if this was what they truly wanted. Of course, that's not what was told to the clients or even expressed in the courtroom. No, the clients were told this was a chance to speak with someone who could help them through the difficult phases of getting espoused. Helping them to handle the discussions with their children. How to accept the changing landscape of friendships, as they would lose some through espouse.

But, in actuality, the State just wanted to make sure there was a true reason to stay together and not some kind of underhanded reason not to uncouple. Was there collusion to try and save money? Easier for them to take care of the kids? Dr. Reed's job was to make sure the couple should get espoused or to recommend that uncoupling should occur.

Teresa sat back in her antique cane chair, looking around her office, admiring her "Victorian-era beachscape" decor. She did not like heavy pieces that contradicted that era's furniture, but she loved mahogany and the fancy intricate wood carving. She spent hours searching online, visiting antique shops, scouring flea markets, and attending auctions looking for the perfect pieces. Her office wasn't terribly large, just big enough to accommodate her and her clients. There was a sofa, plush and textured in white, with a bright purple pattern in velvet. Two dark wooden chairs with ornately carved legs and plush, dark purple cushioning were positioned opposite the sofa. In between the chairs and the sofa, a mahogany coffee table sat on beautifully carved legs. The wall art was all Nantucket seascapes painted by her very talented sister, Deirdre. Hence the "beachscape" decor part of her office design.

The knock on her door brought Teresa out of her daze. "Come in," she called, as she rose from behind her desk, picked up a pad and pencil, and walked over to greet her new clients.

In walked her new couple—Tom and Sara Healy. The first thing Dr. Reed noticed was that they were not holding hands but were keeping each other very close. Okay, nervous, but off to a good start. They might at least believe they want to get espoused.

"Please, come in and be seated on the sofa. I'm Doctor Reed. It is so very nice to meet you."

Sara and Tom each shook Dr. Reed's hand and then proceeded to sit close together on the sofa, Sara more forward on the couch with her hands folded in her lap, while Tom sat back, more relaxed. They both smiled nervously, not sure what to expect since neither one of them had ever been to counseling before.

Dr. Reed sat in one of the chairs opposite the sofa and began, "First, you don't have to be nervous about these sessions. They are confidential and intended to help couples through the emotional roller coaster of getting espoused."

Tom let out his breath and smiled. "Oh, thank goodness. We thought since you were assigned by the state, you would try to convince us to uncouple."

Dr. Reed smiled. *Well, kinda, I'm hired by the state to make sure you really want to espouse.* That was what she thought; what she said was, "No, of course not! I'm here to help couples come together and reorganize themselves to a life of being espoused. This will be a new family paradigm. I want to help you both recognize how family members, especially your children, are impacted by the espouse. I'm to help you gain an understanding of the impact the togetherness is having on the family. It's about creating new rituals since there will be no uncoupling, which has been planned and discussed within the family and expected by society."

She continued, "So, let's begin. Why don't you tell me about yourselves, how you met, your children, and when and how you decided to espouse." Dr. Reed sat back in her chair, opened her pad, and positioned her pencil.

CHAPTER 24

The Separation—Month Three

GWEN SAT IN THE CHAIR at her desk for the first time in a week, with the Healys sitting in front of her.

Funny, she'd thought that when she received good news on Dennis, he would stick to resting while his health continued to improve, and Gwen would be able to concentrate on her caseload.

Instead, her husband had a new strength, a brighter outlook, and was determined to suck the marrow out of life. Oh, they'd been taking it easy, as the doctor said, but they didn't do it hanging around the house. They went for drives. Walks on the Jones Beach boardwalk. Out to dinner in town. To Heckscher Park to visit the art museum or sit on a bench and watch the ducks in the pond. A few days ago, Dennis had taken her hand and said, "I feel it now. Every day I'm getting stronger. I'm going to beat this, Sport."

Gwen smiled at the thought as the Healys got comfortable across from her. When she broke from her trance, she noticed something.

They weren't holding hands.

This is the couple who couldn't keep their hands off of each other four short months ago, right?

She waited for Tom Healy to remember to reach across the arm of the chair and find his wife's hand. But he didn't. He looked ... healthy. Tanned. It was barely March. How the heck had he gotten a tan? Sara wasn't tan, but she had a shine to her eyes. A new haircut. Was she dressing differently too? No more mom jeans and cardigan—skinny jeans, off-the-shoulder blouse, and short boots? *Gosh, they look completely changed.*

Gwen frowned. The last thing she needed was Judge Abraham to be right in ordering the trial separation. She let out a sigh. "And how is separated life treating you two?"

Sara spoke first, without looking at Tom for affirmation. "Fine. As well as can be expected."

Tom nodded. "It's been rough living in separate places and having the kids go back and forth between the different homes. Then there is all the paperwork and financial stuff."

Gwen had warned them about that. For an espouse to go through, there certainly was no shortage of documents to be produced: the financial affidavit, appraisals of property, deeds, and proof of ownership of other assets. But getting the documents shouldn't have been the roughest part of this if two people were truly a good fit for getting espoused.

"I'm sure. And I'm sure it's been very difficult for you living apart," she prompted. When neither of them answered, she pushed forward. "Yes?"

Please, someone, say yes. Otherwise, what am I doing this for? Gwen thought, hanging on their words.

"Oh! Of course," Sara finally said. She gave her husband a fragile smile.

A fake smile?

Tom nodded, too.

Gwen ground her teeth together. "Have you been following all the rules?"

They both nodded.

"Living in separate places?"

Nods.

"No sleepovers?"

Nods.

"Uncouple counseling?"

More nods.

"Sticking to the agreed-upon schedule as far as the children go?"

"Yes," Sara said, looking at Tom. "All except once, but that was because Sam had a stomach bug and Tom was at work. But for the most part, to the letter."

Gwen nodded. Well, that was positive. It showed they were committed to making the espouse happen. Perhaps they were nervous. Maybe they needed a cheerleader to remind them why they were doing this. It could be strange being on a trial separation, having one's life completely upended. "This is good news. Following the rules will definitely help your case. If you continue like this, there's nothing the judge can say to stop your espouse. I think you are doing a great job to make it work for you both."

Tom cleared his throat, and Gwen could see his Adam's apple bob. The couple looked toward each other but not exactly *at* each other. Sara said, her voice soft, "Well. That's wonderful."

"It is!" Gwen said as cheerily as she could, standing up with them and walking them to the front of the house. "You know what I think? I think you two should go out to dinner. Just the two of you. To celebrate how well things are going."

Tom clenched his teeth. Sara's eyes widened. "But ... isn't that against the rules?"

Gwen shook her head. "Certainly, during the separation, fraternization is not encouraged, but there's nothing to say you two can't get together and discuss how things are going. Make sure you're still on the same page."

Gwen put a hand on Sara's shoulder. Sara looked at Gwen doubtfully, then at Tom, who shrugged good-naturedly. "Sure. Makes sense. What do you say, Sara?"

Sara nodded. "Well. Sounds like a great idea, but not tonight though. I have to pick Sam up from Mathletes and Avery up from Scarlet's."

Tom nodded. "All right. Another time then."

Gwen bid them goodbye and then watched from behind a curtain in her office. There was no kiss. No lingering farewells. They simply parted ways, got into separate cars, and drove off.

"Trouble in paradise for the Healys?" called Dennis behind her.

Gwen whirled, feeling her face heat up. Dennis was standing in the doorway, bifocals on, his crossword puzzle book under one arm. "No, of course not," she said, forcing cheer into her voice. "Everything's just fine. Why would you think that?"

Then she looked down and found herself fisting the fabric of the curtain into a tight ball.

Gwen quickly let go and smoothed her clammy hands on the front of her skirt. "Ah, everything will be fine. I'm sure. Now, what would you like for dinner, or should we try that new Mexican restaurant in town?"

CHAPTER 25

What Is Wrong with People?

JUDGE ABRAHAM STARED DOWN at the couple in front of her. A model of what it took to be espoused, they were holding hands under the table as they waited for her verdict.

As usual, it made her sick.

Robert Feinstein stood and held up a copy of the case file. "Well, it's all in here. The Wilsons have followed all the rules, and I don't see any reason why the State should consider enforcing the uncoupling at this time."

The Wilsons huddled closer together as if they were about to withstand a direct hit from a tornado, and they looked at the judge.

It was the little blonde lawyer again. The one Judge Abraham had sent out crying all those months ago. *Susan? Shayna? Something with an S.* Her last name was Boone, but Judge Abraham had taken to calling her Boo since everything sent her running, scared shitless. Now, though, the nickname didn't fit as well. She'd gotten a bit of a backbone in her past few cases. Even just showing up after that first routing showed the kid had spunk.

Judge Abraham hated spunk.

The judge rolled her eyes at Robert while he returned to his seat. Then she sucked on her teeth and pretended to study the case file very carefully. She already knew how she was going to rule, but she liked to draw things out just to see them squirm.

"Fine," she muttered. "Espouse decree granted."

The couple jumped up and hugged and then hugged Boo, who pumped her fist. Judge Abraham watched, unenthused. *Don't get too cocky, there, Boo.*

She watched them leave, arm in arm, thinking they'd probably go and celebrate. *Now you're shackled to one another ... FOREVER. Enjoy.*

Judge Abraham supposed that to some people, that actually sounded good.

Some people with mental conditions, obviously.

Speaking of a man with a mental condition ... "Feinstein!" she barked.

He looked up from the briefcase he was packing. "Yes, Judge. Did I mention that your hair looks lovely today?"

"You did not. But you may." She fluffed it.

"It's very blond. And alluring."

It was almost embarrassing how quickly he skirted to her side, like her own ankle-licking puppy. They'd been working together for years, but only in the past few months had she really noticed him. Robert had gone from the biggest kiss-ass to smarmy and familiar. He was a smart man. Probably knew that with her, flattery did get a person places. Sometimes.

"Don't push it, mister. How's that Healy case coming along? They are doing everything they're supposed to and playing nice in the eyes of the court?"

Feinstein nodded. "Yep. Spic and span."

The judge heaved a big sigh. That was so *boring*. Some people were just so ... pathetic. "So, the separation's in effect, and they're following all the rules?"

"Yep. In order."

The news only annoyed her. The judge slumped in her seat. "What is the deal with all these people coming in here and wanting to espouse? Like theirs is a love for the ages or something. Pass me the barf bag."

Robert gazed at her. "You don't think it's possible to feel so strongly for someone that you can't possibly live without them?"

The judge looked at him like his head was on fire. "Uh. No." She raised an eyebrow. "Do you?"

Robert nodded, a hint of a smile on his face. "Very much. Yes."

"But you're uncoupled."

"As are you. Doesn't mean I can't believe that some people are meant for each other forever."

Her look of mild shock dissolved into a scowl. "What the hell is wrong with you, Feinstein? You work for the State. Your job is to make sure these people uncouple. There should be no forever as far as you're concerned! No wonder these people are so confused! They need someone who will sit and tell them, straight out, that what they're doing is wrong. That they are behaving immaturely and need to get their heads checked. Could you be any weaker? Why can't you see that?"

Robert backed away, his face somber. "I don't know. I just think that if they did everything right, why the heck not? I know that the number of people espousing has been creeping up, almost to fifty percent, especially with the new no-fault espouse law. But ... well, I don't think it makes sense to get worked up about how people want to live their lives and if they want to stay together. If it makes them happy, why not?"

Judge Abraham placed her palms down on the bench and shook her head in disappointment. "Oh my God. Seriously! All this staying-in-love crap! It doesn't make you sick?"

"Frankly, no," Robert said, and Judge Abraham could tell it pained him to disagree with her. "But I mean, we got all types of people in this world. We say love is love, right? Love can't be a bad thing. We say no one should be able to tell us who to love. And I firmly believe that no one should be able to tell us *when* to stop loving, either. If they want to go on past those fifteen years, I say more power to them. They're consenting adults, and they're happy. The only reason I can see for coming between that, Judge? Jealousy. You jealous, Judge?"

Judge Abraham stared at him for a long time. "I'm not jealous of anyone. You get that? No one," she sneered as she pushed away from the bench, gathered up her files, and walked into her chambers.

She really did think Feinstein needed to get that mental condition checked.

CHAPTER 26

Sealed ... Delivered?

KADIR WAS ABLE TO MAKE HIS WAY to the courthouse early
since Riya was going to handle dropping Anaya off at school. Riya had
been spending less and less time at the Stevens's place, with Dennis
giving her more time to spend on the home front. Kadir knew Riya
always felt bad that she couldn't "be there" when her nursing schedule
got too busy, so when it was lighter, she seemed to enjoy her time at
home. When Kadir left, she was poring over a crumpled recipe written
in Hindi, planning on making some big elaborate Indian dish that her
grandmother used to make back in India. Kadir didn't even realize she
knew how to read Hindi.

When he stepped out of his car and locked the door, he took two
steps toward the courthouse and then went back, unclicked the locks,
and retrieved the papers.

The uncoupling documents.

Riya thought he'd already submitted them. He'd told her as much.

Kadir hated lying to her. He knew they'd been working toward this moment for the past fifteen years. But something about this just seemed so ... sudden. He'd needed more time to think about it.

He wasn't sure what amazing thoughts would come to his head in the next few months and make it all right. Make it make sense. Nothing did.

There were few people in the courthouse this early in the morning. *Good. Smooth, Kadir. Make it quick and easy so no one sees and starts some awkward conversation., "So, you are in the uncoupling phase? Congratulations!"* He certainly didn't want to bump into Judge Abraham after her last comments about being irresponsible and late.

Kadir knew he was being irrational. Everyone went through this. It wasn't shameful. It was just life. All he had to do was drop the papers in the slot and go. No big deal.

Still, he kept looking over his shoulder as he walked down the empty hall, his dress shoes clicking on the newly waxed floors. As he opened the manila envelope and looked down at the stack of papers inside, he laughed at himself. The people monitoring the security footage would probably think he was delivering top-secret documents that corresponded to the fate of the nation.

Kadir took one more look to check that the papers were inside. Yep, there they were, including the seventy-five-dollar late fee check that was paper-clipped to the first page.

All ready to go.

Drop it and get on with your life. Easy peasy.

He walked toward the door with the gold placard that said, "UNCOUPLING DOCUMENTS." As expected, it was closed; the office didn't open until nine on weekdays. In the middle of the door was a slot with a sign that said, DEPOSIT UNCOUPLING DOCUMENTS HERE DURING NON-OFFICE HOURS.

Kadir plunged a hand in the pocket of his slacks and, checking once again to make sure no one was watching, strolled, as if out for a walk in the park, casually toward the door. He almost whistled, but he thought that would be overdoing it.

When he got within a few steps of the slot, he broke into a run. He assaulted the slot and, in a frenzy, shoved the papers in with so much force, they probably went sliding across the polished floor of the room inside. Then he quickly backed away and resumed his stroll, this time away from the door.

A moment later, something hit him.

OMG ... I didn't sign them! I was going to do it at home, then in the car, then when I got to the courthouse. He had to get the papers back!

Kadir ran back to the slot, pushed open the metal cover, and peered inside. All he saw was a dark room. He angled himself upward, trying to see the documents. He couldn't see anything.

He pushed his hand in further and felt what was possibly a piece of paper.

What the hell was he doing? Why had he felt he needed to submit these papers so soon? Papers could be submitted up to the day of uncoupling without a person being subjected to jail time, and that w*as* ... what? Four months away? If he was going to have to pay a late fee, why not *really* be late?

Reaching in further, he had almost his entire arm in the slot when he realized that the piece of paper he was touching wasn't a part of his documents. It seemed to be a sign that had been pinned to the wall.

It was hopeless.

Well, if he didn't sign them, that would mean they'd have to return them or call him anyway. *Right?* They wouldn't be able to submit them without the proper signatures.

Kadir sighed and started to pull his arm out of the slot. Pain ripped up his arm as he pulled and pulled.

He was stuck.

Okay, you got it in, you can get it out, he thought, pulling every which way, moving his shoulder one way and then the other, relaxing his shoulder muscles, attempting to mold his skin in different shapes. No matter how he tried, it wasn't working.

Shit.

"Hey, Kadir!" a voice shouted down the hallway. "What's up?"

It was Kevin, another attorney. Of all his friends, Kevin was best known for his ability to make you look like a fool, and he wasn't going to need to try hard now. He stopped in front of Kadir with his venti Starbucks and smiled.

"Got yourself a little stuck, huh?"

Just perfect. "Yeah. Well. I forgot to sign the documents," Kadir said lamely, not making eye contact.

"Wow. You got it stuck in there good. I guess we should call you a janitor?" Kevin said with a very *Man, I'm loving this* smirk on his face as he inspected Kadir's arm closely. "Need to grease you up, huh?"

Kadir nodded, feeling like a total jackass. It was barely seven-thirty in the morning, and he already knew this day was going to suck.

CHAPTER 27

Who Are Our Parents?

AVERY SAT IN STUDY HALL WATCHING Scarlet flirting with Rob Baxter and wondering if the rumors were true.

Scarlet had come in this morning, flushing as red as her name, and proceeded to tell Avery that she and Rob had made out in the closet in the band room for "like five minutes" before the band teacher came in with some kid for a tuba lesson.

Since then, Avery had heard the exact same thing from no fewer than twelve other people.

Was it even a rumor if the person involved in it had told you outright that it did happen? Or the person involved had started spreading it herself?

Scarlet wasn't the most truthful person on earth. She tended to exaggerate a lot. Avery doubted it was really five minutes; maybe it *felt* like five minutes.

Still, she'd always wondered what it would be like to go into some dark, secluded area of the school and lock lips with a boy. What would it feel like? Would she like it?

Rob had used tongue, Scarlet said. And she'd liked it so much, she couldn't wait to do it again. Avery wasn't too sure it sounded all that great.

Forcing her eyes down to the book in front of her—*Watership Down*, snore—she read the same sentence repeatedly as she thought of James. He'd been texting her for months, since before Christmas break, sometimes saying things that sounded like he really liked her.

And then? Then he'd show up and act all ... nervous. It was March now, for goodness' sake!

James had a nice tongue. Avery had seen it every time he blew a bubble with his gum because he couldn't seem to do that without sticking his tongue out. But she was eons away from ever getting to the point where he'd kiss her. The world would probably explode before she ever had her first kiss.

"Hey," a voice said, making her jump.

She looked up and saw James standing over her. She blushed as though he could read her mind.

James pointed to the book. "You didn't finish that yet? The one-pager's due tomorrow."

"Don't remind me," Avery grumbled, closing her book and setting it down. "Why are you here?"

He held up a pink excuse slip. "I told you. Had to miss gym."

Oh, that's right. He'd gone mountain biking with his parents, flipped over a tree root, and got a concussion. He was out of gym class for the week. Lucky guy.

James sat down beside her and motioned to Rob and Scarlet who were sitting close to one another, whispering. "Did you hear?"

Avery rolled her eyes. "Who *didn't* hear?" Then she straightened. *So, he knows about the kiss?* "Um ... what do you think about that?"

He shrugged and leaned back in his chair, putting his knees up against the table. "I think Rob's lucky he didn't get caught. He told me last week he's only one demerit away from suspension."

Avery frowned. It wasn't exactly the answer she was hoping for. "Yeah. I guess. Scarlet was definitely taking a chance, too." She gave him a sideways glance. "Both your parents took you guys mountain biking last weekend? And they went out to the movies the other week. What's going on?"

James shrugged. "Dunno. Whatever it is, it's weird. They actually get along better than they ever did when they were married."

"That *is* weird."

"What about your parents? Is it all doom and gloom with your parents pining for each other?"

Avery shook her head. "No. They are acting weird, too. They seem happier. I know I'm happier. I don't mind going between houses at all—I like the change of scenery. It makes me wonder why they want to get espoused. The only person who might be sad is Sam, but he's a bit of a goober."

James let out a little snort. "You think they might decide to uncouple after all?"

Avery crossed her fingers and smiled. "Fingers crossed."

James shook his head. "The first few months, my parents were like that. They were dating new people, really happy and just ... I don't know ... alive. And now, here they are, seeing each other every day, having sleepovers together ... they even broke up with whoever they were dating and seem to prefer each other's company. I think they might even be planning a family trip to Disney together."

"Really? Oh, geez," Avery said, watching as Rob and Scarlet put their heads together. She decided that was the problem. Didn't matter how close people got; it was sometimes still impossible to tell what the other person would do. And clearly, that had not changed in fifteen years. "Sounds like your parents should've gotten espoused instead of mine."

James scrubbed both hands over his face. "Don't even joke about that."

CHAPTER 28

Father and Son Time

DENNIS LOOKED UP from an office copy of *People* and smiled at Terrell, who was looking at the television and frowning. It was another political piece, with a ridiculous headline at the bottom scroll bar made to turn heads.

"I remember," Dennis said with a grin, "the good old days. When news reporters actually tried to be objective."

Terrell muttered, "It gets my blood pressure up."

"Trust me," Dennis said, shaking his head. "It's not worth it, stewing over he said, she said. I tell you, the truth is somewhere in the middle, and it isn't all that interesting. Just live your life."

Terrell turned away from the television and grinned at him. "Wiser words were never spoken."

Dennis was damn glad to see Terrell again. He usually came down from Boston once a month, but he'd been down twice this month, agreeing to take Dennis to his monthly oncologist appointments. Gwen always went above and beyond for her son when he showed up, trying to set up special activities the boys could do together, now that Dennis had more energy. This weekend, she'd made reservations at Meehan's of Huntington for lunch, and they were going to catch opening day of the Yankees. "I'll go as long as he promises not to wear his Red Sox cap," Dennis had grumbled.

"Who me?" Terrell answered, shrugging innocently. "I'm a Yankees fan for life."

A door opened, and a nurse appeared. "Mr. Stevens? Dr. Patel will see you now."

The two of them went through the door into an examination room. When they were left alone, Dennis hopped up on the examination table. He'd been going for his radiation treatments and blood tests bi-weekly, taking his immunotherapy pills, and he was getting into the groove. Amazing what a little bit of energy could do for you. In fact, he didn't want to jinx things, but he hadn't felt this good since he was in his forties.

As they waited, they spoke a little about the Yankees' chances for making the playoffs this year, about Terrell's job, and about how things were going up in Beantown now that he was working for one of the most prestigious firms in Boston, specializing in employment law. Terrell had a girlfriend, an attorney named Amanda, and Gwen had been begging him to bring her down.

"I'm going to, I'm going to!" Terrell said, throwing up his hands. "I know she's really looking forward to Mom's thorough inspection to see if she meets with the old Gwen Stevens approval."

Dennis laughed. "Yeah. Personally, I'd rather face a firing squad." He grinned. "She does it because you're her only baby, and she loves you."

Terrell sat back in his chair and pulled his Yankees cap low over his eyes. "I'm twenty-five."

He grinned. "Shh. Don't tell her that."

"Well. She gave me hell when I told her we'd moved in together," Terrell said, shaking his head. "What she doesn't get is that even though we're making good money, we have law school student loans to pay off, and rents in downtown Boston aren't exactly cheap."

Dennis laughed. He'd met Gwen when she was a couple of years older than Terrell was now. Back then, she'd been going through the same thing; trying to afford rent in her new apartment and paying off her law school loans. It hadn't been easy, and knowing how college costs had skyrocketed, he doubted it was any easier now.

Dr. Patel came in and shook both of their hands, his wrist somewhat limp. "Good morning," he said stiffly, avoiding looking at either Terrell or Dennis directly.

Dennis knew something was not quite right the second the doctor walked through the door. Dr. Patel wasn't usually a man of many smiles, but he looked even more somber and business-like than usual as he scanned Dennis's file.

"Is something wrong, Doc?" Dennis asked, catching the way Terrell's smile slowly faded the moment he asked.

"Well, there's a bit of concern in your bloodwork. Your white blood cells have fallen off dramatically."

Terrell gripped the arms of the chair. "What does that mean?"

The doctor shook his head. "Nothing on its own. It's a cause for concern. Probably nothing to worry about, but I'd like to do a CAT scan to be sure."

Dennis nodded. *Nothing to worry about, nothing to worry about, nothing to worry about.* He repeated it to himself, but the words didn't have the calming effect he'd hoped for. And just like that, he slumped back against the examination table and began to feel lightheaded and out of breath for the first time in two months.

"Dad? You okay?" Terrell asked in concern.

"Son," he rasped, putting his hands on his knees to steady them from shaking. "Would you mind terribly if we watched the baseball game from home today?"

CHAPTER 29

Dinner with Friends

JESSICA FROWNED AT YET *another* text from that leech, Marco, deleted it, and popped her phone into her bag as Michael ordered her a craft beer.

They were sitting at the bar at Meehan's of Huntington on a busy Friday night. Karaoke would be later. Michael had joked that he was going to get her up there so they could do a duet of "Still the One" by Shania Twain. Their wedding song.

"That wasn't James, was it?" Michael asked, pointing at her phone.

Jessica shook her head. Unfortunately, Marco couldn't get it out of his head that the two of them weren't destined for one another. He'd gotten too serious, too soon, and he texted her all the time. He was like a forty-year-old stalker! She was close to blocking his number, but since he was a pediatrician, he had been very helpful when James had endured his concussion last weekend.

She looked at Michael. "Why? Are you concerned about James?"

Michael shrugged. "He's been unusually pensive. I hope it's not a result of last weekend."

"Oh." Jessica wasn't sure. But she'd seen the way James and Cara were looking at their parents every time they walked into a room together. Both looked confused and concerned. She had to think it must be confusing to them, and the last thing she wanted to do was confuse them.

Besides, she wasn't sure what she and Michael were doing.

Right now, they were doing what they hadn't done the last few years of their marriage: enjoy each other's company.

But it just made sense. After the downfall of Marco, she'd realized that Michael had so many qualities she admired. She'd begun to see the things she once thought of as failings as good qualities. The way he couldn't make a decision without consulting her first. The way he constantly worried about the children. The way he texted her each night before she went to sleep, just to say good night.

Jessica had heard, too, through her children, that Michael had broken up with his blonde co-ed. James had said it was a good thing because the one time she'd come over to meet them, all she did was talk to James about how much fun it was getting wasted at frat parties. Jessica had brought it up, and Michael had immediately agreed to keep her away from their children. After that, it'd just fizzled.

Michael checked his phone. "They're late."

"Give them time. They have to come all the way across town."

"Yeah, but since when are they ever late?"

Jessica nodded, scanning the crowd gathered at the front of the restaurant. That was true. Tom was a precise, to-the-letter man. They were always on time.

Michael leaned forward, a mischievous glint in his eyes, and said,

"Truthfully, I wouldn't mind at all if they—"

He stopped when the door opened and Sara walked in, leaving Jessica to wonder what he had been planning to say. *He wouldn't mind at all if it were just the two of us?*

Shrugging it off, she jumped from her stool and embraced her friend, looking back at the door. "Where's Tom?"

Sara shrugged.

"You came in separate cars?"

"Yes," Sara said as Michael vacated his stool, allowing her to sit. She pulled off her jacket and slid up onto the seat. "You know the judge ordered us a trial separation?"

"Oh, right," Jessica said. She had heard from James, but she hadn't expected them to follow it so stringently. "How are things going with that? You look fabulous, by the way. I love your hair."

Sara swiped a dark strand of hair behind her ear and was about to answer when Tom breezed through the door. He looked different, too, and it took a while for Jessica to understand why. He was tan. He was normally buttoned-up, but now, his shirt was unbuttoned at the throat, revealing a bit of his bronzed chest. *Did he go on a vacation?* Tom shook Michael's hand and hugged Jessica. Jessica watched as he leaned in and gave Sara an awkward kiss with them both turning their heads as if they weren't sure whether to aim for the lips or the cheek. It was so bizarre that Jessica had to look away.

Yeesh. They look like one-night-stands who met up again by accident.

Michael pressed into Jessica's side, his arm wrapped around her waist in a way that made her feel treasured, as Tom ordered Sara a Long Island iced tea.

"Tom," Sara said, glaring at him. "I can order for myself. I was looking forward to having one of those craft beers."

Tom frowned. "We've been coming here for ages, and you always get a—"

"Yes, but I came here last week, and I tried a couple of the craft beers." Sara's voice was clipped.

Tom raised his finger to the bartender and corrected the order as Jessica and Michael exchanged glances. A quiet tension ensued, broken when the hostess came and announced their table was ready.

Sara pushed off her chair and strode ahead without even waiting for Tom.

Jessica looked at Michael and silently rubbed her upper arms as if to say: *Is it chilly in here, or is it just me?* He clenched his teeth and helped her from her chair, keeping his hand on the small of her back until they'd reached their table. Jessica hoped she wouldn't have to endure another two hours of bickering.

"So, how is separated life?" Jessica asked when she set her beer down in front of her. "Really hard?"

Sara nodded and opened her menu. "Oh. Yes. It's a lot to get used to. I think we're managing it, but it was difficult at first."

"But," Tom said, burying his face in his menu, "you have been going out for beers, so it can't be all that bad."

Sara snapped the menu closed. "What's that supposed to mean?"

Tom shrugged innocently. "Just that I haven't even had the time to gallivant, what with my job and the kids' schedules and—"

"I wasn't gallivanting! I went out for a couple of beers with some of my friends from work!"

Oh, God, Jessica thought, bracing herself against the edge of the table. *Change the subject.*

Michael must have thought the same thing because he came to the rescue before she could think of an appropriate and safe topic. "Have you tried the Bavarian butter-baked pretzels? They come with beer cheese. I hear they are very good."

The Healys turned to him and stared as if he had asked whether they had traveled to the moon lately. It was like they'd forgotten where they were ... out with friends. Sara reached for her beer and shook her head, a blush crawling over her cheeks. "No, I haven't. I usually just get a salad."

More tense silence. Finally, Tom closed his menu, took a chug of his drink, and said, "You two really look like you're enjoying the uncoupled life, huh?"

Michael looked at Jessica and scratched his chin. "Yeah. Sure. It's ... good."

"I mean, you said you were really into it the last time we saw you. At Starbucks?" Tom prodded.

Sara added, "You said you heartily recommended it, Michael."

Michael closed his menu and grabbed his drink, taking a swig. "Yes, I did, and—"

Sara looked at Jessica. "You said that it was such a refreshing change of pace to look past your comfort zone and see a new point of view."

Jessica hesitated. *Geez, had Sara remembered everything we said, word for word? I really need to be more careful before I speak.* "Er, yes, I did say that."

"I think that's why this trial has been helpful to us. It gives us a taste of what you were talking about," Sara went on, not looking at Tom. Instead, she looked into her beer and drained the whole glass in two massive gulps.

Great, is Sara becoming an alcoholic now? Fantastic.

"Yes, but once you have that taste ... you realize that maybe you don't want the entire entrée," Jessica said lamely, looking at Michael.

Tom said, "Then you take a taste of something else, right? You must be having a good time broadening your horizons, exploring new things that each other might not have gotten into, right?" He looked around, trying to find a waiter. "Avery told us that you took James mountain biking last weekend, huh, Michael?"

"We all did that, actually," Jessica said, gnawing on her lip. "As a family."

Tom whipped his head around to look at both Jessica and Michael. "Ah."

Michael shrugged. "Jess wanted to go but wasn't sure about how to get to the trail. It was fortunate because James did end up hitting his head. So, it was a good thing we were all together."

Jess laughed and put her hand over her ex-husband's. Realizing her mistake, she quickly put her hand back in her lap. "It worked out for the best having Michael there. He was able to console Cara while I tended to James."

Her laughter faded when she realized that Sara and Tom were staring at her with mouths slightly open.

"Ah," Tom said again.

Having finished her drink, Sara picked up her water glass and started chewing on the ice cubes, crunching noisily as the waiter finally came to take their order. All four hoped the food would arrive quickly.

CHAPTER 30

Just Like Grandma Used to Make

RIYA LEANED OVER the stovetop and tasted her concoction.

She winced.

This was her grandma Shivani's recipe, brought all the way over from India, a tried, true, and treasured dish that had delighted generations. Riya couldn't quite remember her grandmother's rendering bringing tears to her eyes the way it was doing now. Shivani was probably rolling over in her grave.

"Too much curry powder," she gagged, running the faucet and getting herself a glass of water.

Riya checked her phone. *Great.* Kadir would be home in fifteen minutes to this inedible mess that she'd spent practically all day trying to make. Of course, he wanted to uncouple. She wasn't like Grandma Shivani or her own mother, who'd both uncoupled like normal people. They both would be unhappy about her thinking of espouse. "Throwing tradition out the window," Riya heard them saying. She was a failure as a homemaker, a mother, a wife, a daughter, and granddaughter.

Stop, she told herself, thinking of what her grandmother would do about her food mess. Her grandmother was always coming up with these recipes because she wasn't afraid to take risks. This could be fixed.

Reaching into the pantry, she grabbed some more coconut milk. Riya poured it in and, reluctantly, took another small taste.

Not as terrible. *There's hope for this dinner yet. I will conquer you!*

As she quietly celebrated her coup, she heard the door slam. Riya looked at the time on the microwave. Anaya, as punctual as ever, back from her after-school soccer practice on the late bus. She smiled. Even if she lost Kadir, she'd always have Anaya, her good, well-behaved, dutiful little girl.

She expected a "Hi, Mom," but there was none.

"Anaya?" she called as Anaya appeared in the doorway to the mudroom. The frown on her daughter's face told Riya everything: her only child had had a bad day.

Anaya stalked in, shrugged off her loaded backpack, and threw it on the ground in the foyer.

"Your backpack doesn't go there," Riya reminded her, a bit surprised at this behavior. "Pick it up, please."

She expected Anaya to quietly return and comply. But she didn't. She stalked into the living room and threw herself on the couch with a deep scowl on her face.

Riya had been getting ready to ask her to set the table, but she held back. Wiping her hands on a dishrag, she walked over to her daughter and sat at her feet. "Hello? Since when do you ignore me? I asked you to pick up your backpack."

Anaya crossed her arms and faced the wall.

Riya waved a hand in front of her daughter's face. "Anaya, what's wrong with you? You've had a bad attitude ..."

"What's wrong with *me*?" Anaya erupted, slamming her fists down on her thighs. "*I've* had a bad attitude? You guys are the ones who are always yelling at each other! It's enough to make me sick!"

Riya froze, stunned by her daughter's outbreak. The last time she'd seen her like this, Anaya had accidentally gotten a ballpoint pen smudge on her American Girl doll's face. "We don't—"

"You do! Of course, you do! You argue about visitation, about who is staying in the condo and who is going to the new place, about money and bank accounts ... everything!"

Riya swallowed. Yes, they had been ... not arguing, she thought ... but *strenuously discussing* all the necessary arrangements that would need to be made during the pending uncoupling. Their voices might have been raised, but ... they weren't yelling. Were they?

She moved to swipe away a long lock of her daughter's dark hair that had fallen from her ponytail and into her face. "Now, Anaya—"

Anaya swatted her mother away. "No! I don't want to hear it." She jumped up and stood in front of her, shaking in rage. "I can't wait until you guys uncouple because then I won't have to listen to you argue anymore!"

Then she rushed up the stairs to her room and slammed the door, making the whole house shake.

Riya stood there for a moment, staring after her. Quietly, she climbed the stairs and tried the door.

It was locked. Anaya never locked the door.

Riya knocked.

"Go away," Anaya mumbled, her voice muffled by a pillow.

Sighing, Riya went back downstairs in time to hear the garage door opening. Kadir was home. She did have one topic to talk to him about, one unpleasant thing that might upset them both. Although, uncoupling shouldn't be unpleasant. They had gotten married knowing they would uncouple, filed the uncoupling updates every year, bought the second home. Riya had received a call from the filing office regarding the uncoupling documents, about an "issue" with the documents they'd submitted earlier that month. She'd put off bringing it up with Kadir for a few days.

As Riya walked into the kitchen, though, a loud, grating alarm sounded above her. Smoke wafted up, and the smell of burning food assaulted her nostrils.

In a panic, she ran to the kitchen and saw that the meal from Grandma Shivani's recipe was on fire. Not just blackened, or smoking, or burnt. Flames were shooting up, almost hitting the overhead fan.

Riya let out a frantic cry. Digging her hand into a potholder, she pulled the pot off the stove, threw it into the sink, and ran the water.

Just as Kadir came in.

His face was, in a word, disgusted. "What the hell happened?"

But Riya couldn't answer. She knew they'd probably end up ordering pad thai again for the fifth time that month. That was what Kadir expected. That was why he would never want her, the incompetent wife that she was.

She sat down at the kitchen table, put her face in her hands, and stated bluntly, "Call for pad thai. Otherwise, there's no dinner."

CHAPTER 31

Rules to Live By

SAM HEALY SAT ON THE BLEACHERS in the band room, looking around at the faces of the other kids. A couple of them he knew from school, but most were from other schools in the area. Still, they all looked normal, just like him. Unlike what Avery seemed to think, none of them had weird nervous tics or horns protruding from their heads.

Sam hadn't been able to get Avery to come to COEIP. It'd been court-ordered, but in the end, they'd been told that it was only "strenuously" recommended. Avery had said she needed to do something for cheerleading. The real reason? She was afraid that Scarlet and all the other plastics she called friends would make fun of her. What a lemming.

Sticking his chin out as if to show he didn't care, he noticed some of the kids pulling chairs from the back and arranging them in a circle.

He helped do the same, sitting next to a girl who was probably a little older than him. "Hi," she said to him with a smile.

Sam stared at her, open-mouthed. She was clearly one of the students from the other schools Ms. Kim mentioned attended these sessions. After all, most people from this school didn't say hi to him. Especially girls. Girls usually ignored him, except Cara, who he always thought was playing with him. Every time Cara saw him, she'd say, really loudly so everyone could hear, "How's your parents' espouse going, Sammy?"

"Uh, hi."

"Your first time?" she asked.

His eyes widened. Not only had she said hi to him, but now she wanted to carry on a conversation? He nodded. Was it obvious how much of a newbie he was?

"I knew it. I haven't seen you around. I mean, I haven't seen you here before. I don't go to this school. I just come to the support group." She put out her hand to shake. "I'm Samantha. Sam."

He blinked. *Whoa! Maybe she's a female version of me from a parallel universe.* He shook her hand and said, "Uh. I'm Sam too."

"Wow. Really?" She giggled.

He nodded and let out a weird guffaw. "Yeah. I've been Sam all my life."

Oh, God, that was dumb. Could I be any lamer?

She didn't seem to notice how silly or ridiculous he was, though. She smiled and said, "I really like it here. It's cool. You get to talk about what you're feeling. Some people think that's stupid, but I don't. I'd rather be here than shaking pom poms or whatever."

Sam raised an eyebrow. He thought all girls wanted to be cheerleaders. "Really?"

She nodded. "Definitely. There are better ways to spend your free time, in my opinion. My parents went through the espouse process three years ago."

"Three? Oh, wow."

She nodded. "Yeah. I guess you'd probably call me a COEIP alumni. They didn't go through with it, though. My mother wanted to espouse, but as it turns out, my father really wanted to uncouple. At first, my dad went along with my mom to get espoused, but the uncoupling counselor discovered the truth. So, they ended up getting uncoupled like most people."

"And it worked out okay? Are you okay?"

She started playing with the ends of her blond hair. "Yes, I'm great! Life is fine. My parents are happy, but I keep coming back here because I love it so much!"

Okay, Sam thought. *She loves it? Seriously? That sounds a little weird.* He thought coming here to talk with people who were experiencing the same thing could be helpful. He didn't think he'd come to love it.

"Are your parents espoused?" Sam the girl asked.

"Not yet. But they want to be. They're having a trial separation right now."

"Ohhhh," she said knowingly. "Trial seps can be hard. When my parents did that, it was a tough time. My dad should have just fessed up in the beginning."

Sam nodded, glad to have someone who understood. Talking to Avery was like talking to a wall. Last time he'd tried to talk to her about the espouse, she'd thrown a pair of scissors at him.

Maybe his parents would decide to uncouple like Sam the girl's parents. That would be amazing. Mom was spending more time on how she looked, she was going out more with friends, and working too! Sam was so confused. *Why can't my parents just talk about it and figure it out already?!*

Suddenly, the door flew open, and in pranced Ms. Kim, her bright red, unruly hair bouncing around her face. She wore a bright pink flowing dress that went down to her ankles, with bright yellow sunflowers splashed across the dress. It reminded Sam of her office with all the smiley faces.

Ms. Kim moved to one of the empty chairs, flounced up her dress, and sat down, speaking cheerily, "Hello, my little chickadees! This is the Children of Espoused Intervention Program! For those of you who don't know me, my name is Ms. Kim!! If you were looking for free donuts, you have come to the wrong place!"

Only Sam the girl laughed. Everyone else stared blankly at her.

"All right, before we start the introductions, let's join hands and sing our group song. Sam, will you lead us?"

Sam had a momentary jolt before he realized she was referring to Sam the girl, who grabbed his hand and squeezed it. He reached over and took the hand of the guy next to him, feeling a little pathetic, as Sam the girl broke out in a song. Sam tried to follow along so he could sing the verse next time, but the only thing he got was, *we will overcome and live in peace.*

Ms. Kim clapped her hands. "Now. As this is the start of a new session, I want to give an overview of our aim for this group. First of all, know that this is a safe place to discuss anything and everything you want, whether or not it relates to your parents' espouse. Additionally, you are always welcome to attend these meetings even after your parents espouse." Then she caught Sam the girl's eye and added, "Or decide to uncouple after all!"

She reached into a red folder and pulled out a pile of papers, which she motioned to the girl next to her to pass around. Sam got his and read it eagerly:

Topics to Discuss

1. What's Happening with My Family? Finding comfort and relief from the anxiety of what is happening in your life!

2. Facing Anger! How to recognize angry feelings! Learn it's okay to be mad that your parents are staying together but not to hurt others when angry!

3. Journey from Anger to Sadness! How to deal with the sadness phase of grief in the espouse process!

4. I Am Not Alone! Realize you are not alone and that it is okay to ask for help!

5. It's Not My Fault! You did not cause this! This is an adult problem between parents!

6. Telling Parents How You Feel! Help pick the words and learn how to talk to your parents!

7. Forgiveness! Learn to forgive your parents and take responsibility for your own actions!

8. Loving Your Parents! Learn that your parents still love you and each other! Learn to express your love to both parents without taking sides!

9. Moving On: Growing Up and Closer Together! Realize life goes on after espouse, and you will have a healthy and happy future!

Yes. Yes! This was what Sam was looking for. An iron-clad, easy-to-follow plan for getting over his parents' psychosis. He found himself nodding as he read. Even Avery would benefit from this. Of course, she'd probably look at it and say, *Whoa, someone was a little too generous with the exclamation usage. Need to reel that in a little, huh?*

Sam the girl leaned over to him and smiled. "Sounds good, doesn't it?"

He nodded. It sounded better than good. If this was what he had to do to get over his parents' espouse, he'd survive. And hey, Sam the girl was living proof that he could get past this. Maybe this wasn't the end of the world after all. He was ready to let the healing begin.

CHAPTER 32

The Separation—Month Four

SARA SMILED as she stepped out of Bloomingdales at the Walt Whitman Mall, her arms laden with packages.

She'd always wanted to do this. But she'd always felt guilty going off on a shopping spree just for herself when her husband was locked in his office all day and the kids needed so much of her time for school, activities, et cetera. For the past fourteen years, most of her shopping trips had been for the family. She'd bought most of her clothes at Target or Old Navy while shopping for the kids.

She felt a little thrill travel the length of her spine when she thought of the Louis Vuitton pumps she'd just purchased. A day after the trial separation began, she had bought a pair of $250 Coach pumps, and she loved all the compliments she'd received. These new Louis Vuitton shoes were definitely a splurge at $1,400, especially for something she wouldn't wear every day. Lime green with a big silver buckle on the top, they were a statement piece; a piece people couldn't help but notice.

She couldn't wait to wow people and show them just how well she was getting along on her own. That's what many of their uncoupled friends had said when they first heard that she and Tom were going to espouse. *Oh, poor girl, it's too bad since you are so dependent on Tom. This separation must be difficult for you, doing so much on your own!* No one ever thought that maybe, just maybe, they were in love?

Now, things seemed reversed. Tom had always been so strong. But when the separation came up, he'd suddenly dissolved into a clingy, wimpy mess. Where was the strong man she admired, the guy she so depended on?

It only took about two months to become more in charge of her life. To stop picking up the phone to text Tom to ask permission to buy something, what to cook for dinner, what to watch on TV.

But, after all, she was only doing what Dr. Reed had suggested in their last therapy session. She had told them to work on healthy uncouple activities, all based on the following criteria:

- Is something you can do separately
- Is something you can do regularly (separately)
- Is enjoyable for that particular individual
- Is something that allows you not to feel guilty about and have no problem communicating to others in a healthy and productive way

Well, Sara enjoyed shopping! And it seemed it met all the healthy uncoupling activity criteria.

The kids seemed happy, too. Well, Avery seemed glad about it. Sam, her sensitive boy, had been adjusting, especially since joining in his weekly espouse counseling group at school. They all seemed to be handling the separation very well ... exceptionally well.

Sara believed another two months of separation would not be hard to get through. She was thinking of this as she went into Starbucks and ordered a latte. She should be at home finishing her latest article for work, but it would be there when she got home.

Sara ordered a muffin, too, and sat down, thinking of the phone call she'd received from Tom after they'd gone out to eat at Meehan's a few weeks ago. He'd been mopey, like a little kid. He'd said he felt like she was growing too distant. Sara had assured him that she loved him, explained that she was just doing what was required by the trial separation, and suggested he think more positive.

Sara knew Tom didn't have many friends, but he should expand his horizon a little. In the past four months, she'd met several times with friends for lunch at Meehan's, and she'd even flirted with a man in the supermarket who'd asked for her number! Sara told him she was busy as she didn't want to explain that she wasn't uncoupled, but the shiver of excitement, of possibility, had traveled through her body. She hadn't felt anything like that in a long time.

When she finally did go back to Tom, maybe she'd have all of that out of her system.

As Sara finished her muffin, she hoped she would, anyhow. She'd already gained five pounds.

Across town, Tom showed up at the middle school to pick up the kids. As he drove, he was thinking about Sara. She'd blown him off, yet again, during his nightly phone call. She always seemed to be too busy to talk to him. And when they did the weekend switch? It was very awkward and very quick. Sara barely had time to update him on the kids' schedule or what had happened while they were with her.

How had things come to this?

Tom knew what might have started it. About a month after the trial separation was put in place, he'd decided to take a vacation, by himself, to Aruba. It was something he'd always wanted to do, but Sara, being fair-skinned, never wanted to go on a beach vacation—she preferred Disney or hiking the mountains. Active things. Tom spent the entire time on the beach, sitting in the sun, doing absolutely nothing. What he thought would be so relaxing had just been sad. He spent the whole time thinking about his family and wishing they were with him.

But Sara? When he returned, she was different. She'd gotten herself a new outfit, one for her new job, as well as a haircut and color. She looked different ... like the Sara he'd first met at Hofstra.

Was Sara enjoying this separation? She used to annoy him during the day with questions about everything. *Avery's teacher called, do you want to call the school or should I? I'm sending Sam to his friend's house, is six o'clock too late to pick him up? I was thinking of a light gray paint for the laundry room, is that okay?* Now she didn't touch base with him at all.

Tom was becoming concerned.

But how should I bring that up to her? He was all-in, willing to do whatever it took to get back together. To be espoused.

Avery was still on the field practicing her cheerleading drills for spring sports, but Tom made it to the band wing just as the COEIP session was ending. He peered in the window and saw Sam talking to a girl. The two of them were smiling, and Sam had that goofy, obsessively wide-eyed look he got whenever he really liked something. Tom was happy to see he had made a friend. He thought Sam was still in that phase of his life where talking to girls was not cool yet.

In a daze, he stepped back just as the door opened and kids started to filter out, and he stumbled right into someone behind him. He started to apologize before he even looked up, but once he did, his voice died. It was a woman in yoga pants and a Soul Cycle zippered jacket, with a blond ponytail, and she was making a face like he'd mortally wounded her.

"Oh, God, I'm so sorry," he said, stammering. "I didn't see you."

"It's okay," she said, straightening up with a kind smile. "Just a foot. I have another one."

Sam bounded out with the girl right at his heels. The girl went right to the woman Tom had stepped on, and the four of them stood there, silently. Tom's mind was a complete jumble. *What is with you? It's just a very pretty, very nice woman. You're in a trial separation, not uncoupled. Get a grip!*

Tom gently punched Sam on the shoulder. "Uh, ... Sam? How was the session?"

Sam hitched a shoulder coolly. "Fine."

The pretty blonde stared at Tom with mouth agape. "Your son's name is Sam? That's my daughter's name."

Tom raised an eyebrow. "Ah. So, you and your husband are getting espoused?"

"No, actually, we are uncoupled," she said with a shy smile. "It's a funny story. The judge ordered a trial separation for six months, and while we were apart, my husband decided he didn't want to go through with the espouse after all."

Actually, that wasn't funny at all. "That must've been hard for you."

She shrugged her shoulders. "That was three years ago. I'm over it." She put her hands on her daughter's shoulders. "This one. I don't know what to tell you. She no longer is required to attend these meetings, but she loves it so much, she doesn't want to give it up."

Sam the girl blushed. "Hey, can you show me your school's trophy display? Our school's isn't nearly as big!" The two kids left to check out the display case, leaving Tom and Sam the girl's mom standing together. Tom plunged his hands into his pockets and tried to think of something to say.

"I'm Cheryl, by the way," she said, extending her hand. "My daughter doesn't attend this school. She just attends the support group."

He shook it. "Tom. I didn't realize kids from other schools attended as well. I guess that makes sense to have a larger group to support each other."

"So, you're in the process of getting espoused, huh?" Cheryl asked, hitching her little backpack-style purse more comfortably on her back.

Tom looked over at the kids and bit at his cheek. "Yes." Then he looked back at Cheryl and shrugged. "That is what we are supposed to be doing."

CHAPTER 33

What Am I Feeling?

JESSICA AND MICHAEL WALKED together into Starbucks. Michael was reminiscing about the time they'd gone up to Maine and gotten very sick on the whale watching boats. "The only thing that saved me was that hot tub on the balcony!" laughed Jessica.

"The only thing that saved me was what we did in that hot tub," Michael said, squeezing her side. As Michael opened the door for Jessica, she ran straight into Sara Healy, who was tossing a muffin wrapper and latte cup into the trash.

Sara continued to look better every time Jessica saw her. She'd been putting on weight, which was a good thing in Sara's case because Jessica had always thought Sara was much too thin. And she'd gotten her hair cut again, this time an even shorter, spiky 'do with burgundy highlights, which made her look years younger.

"Oh, hi, Sara! I love the new 'do," Jessica said, inspecting Sara's bags as she gathered them into her arms. She'd really been through the shops today; Jessica thought she might have had a bag from every store in the mall. "Shopping spree?"

Sara smiled, her eyes darting between the two of them. "Yes. Felt like a long time since I'd treated myself."

"Well, good for you," Michael said. "Need any help taking those bags to your car?"

Sara shook her head. "No, I'm good, but thank you! Well, I need to rush! Bye," she said, heading for the door.

As soon as the door closed behind Sara, Jessica turned to Michael, her eyes wide. "Whoa. What do you think of that?"

Michael approached the counter and ordered their two coffees. "I think that the separation is definitely having a positive effect on Sara."

"Her, yes. I think she might be enjoying it a little too much, don't you think?"

Michael swiped his card and nodded thoughtfully as they walked to the other counter to wait for their drinks. "Maybe. Tom looked a little lost when we saw him for dinner. Remember?"

Jessica laughed. "How could I forget? He was like a deer in the headlights. He's probably looking at Sara like, *Is this my wife?* She's changed a lot. But he was tan. Looked like he'd just gotten back from vacation, so maybe he's enjoying himself, too."

They got their coffees, put in cream and sugar, and sat down.

"So, do you think they'll go through with it?" Jessica asked.

"What? The espouse?" Michael crossed his arms. "Yeah. Eventually. They were so in love. I can't imagine that has changed. I think they are both just enjoying a little freedom. I'm sure it will get old before the six-month separation is over."

"True." Jessica took a slow sip from her coffee then pulled back. Too hot yet. She removed the lid to let it cool down. "I was thinking; their hearing is in two months. I'd really like to show them our support."

"Yeah. We should be there."

We, Jessica thought. *We're uncoupled, so why do I keep including him in everything I do?*

Even so, every time one of them mentioned they might do something, the other one inevitably found a reason to tag along. Jessica smiled. "Great," she said. "Though I do feel like they'll be missing out."

Michael glanced at her. "How so?"

"Well. Look at us. Uncoupling changed everything for us. We were so miserable, and now everything is working very well, we are both happy, the kids are doing great ... it's like ..."

"Kind of like we're best friends without the benefits?" he offered.

"Yes! I mean, it's ... good, you know?" She smiled brightly at him.

"Yeah. I was just thinking that." He beamed at her.

It was good. Except as Michael said, no benefits. Best friends didn't kiss each other, lived separately, and took care of the kids separately—well, most of the time. And after they had all their adventures together, she'd go to sleep, alone. *Other than that, it's perfect.*

Jessica looked across the table at Michael. They smiled at each other. Her smile slowly faded as his eyes drifted down to her lips. He licked his lips. She knew him well enough to know he was thinking of kissing her.

But what if we took that extra step and added that back in?

If they did, they might as well have been espoused. Right? And then they'd both have to admit that uncoupling was a mistake.

No, they had fought all the time, at least the last few years of marriage. Uncoupling had been good for them.

Then why do I miss him so much when he's not around? Her eyes swept over him, and she remembered with a thrill what it was like to be intimate with him. She couldn't deny it; she missed that. She wanted it again. And fifteen years with Michael had taught her his body language. He wanted it, too.

A sick feeling settled in the pit of Jessica's stomach, and she quickly moved away from him, darting her eyes out the window. "Do you think it's going to rain? I'd hate for James's opening day of baseball to get ruined."

CHAPTER 34

Spring Is in the Air

IT WAS A CRAZY, WARM DAY. Almost seventy in early March. All the kids were outside for lunch. James Baum watched Avery sitting on the curb with Scarlet. Their sleeves were pushed up so they could capture some sun on their pale limbs. Rob was there, too, his arm wrapped around Scarlet's waist—they'd officially started going out two weeks ago. Their making out in the band closet was old news now; James wouldn't put it past the two of them to be doing a lot more than that.

Nasty.

James looked at Avery. He'd certainly like to kiss her and was trying not to imagine doing anything else. Really, he just wanted to ... he wasn't sure. Climb inside her head and get to know her? Be close to her? She could be nice when she wasn't all wrapped up in Instagram or Snapchat, keeping up with what Scarlet and Rob and the rest of those people were doing. The past few months of texting had shown him her soft side, a side he wanted to know.

What if he told her how he felt, and she turned him into her Instagram toy-boy? A Kardashian-type boy-user to build up her fame?

James didn't want to be that. Ever.

Thus, their relationship had been nothing but texting. For five solid months.

Taking a breath, he reached into his pocket, pulled out his mirrored sunglasses, and pushed them up over his nose.

Then he walked up to the three of them, hands tucked in the pockets of his jeans. "What's up?"

Scarlet and Rob, lost in each other, barely noticed him, but Avery looked up from her phone and gave him a smile that made up for it. She shuffled over on the curb so he could sit beside her. "How are you?"

"Good." James saw that she was scrolling through her selfies. *Wow, she has a lot of selfies.*

Avery lifted up her phone in front of them and squeezed in close to him. She smelled like vanilla candy. "Come on."

He looked up at the camera; she snapped the picture, then inspected it. Shook her head. Held the camera up again.

"Another," she said.

After about two more tries, she finally got the right picture and started thumbing in the words to go with her post: *Hangin with friends in this great weather! #lunchtime #dontmakemegobackinside*

James frowned. Scarlet was the worst about documenting her every move on social media, but Avery wasn't far behind. It was like they were in some kind of competition over who had the most fabulous life. He waited for her to finish. As she did, Rob and Scarlet stood up and wiped off their jeans. They said "See ya" in unison and walked away, pinkies linked.

James looked after them, suddenly aware that he was now alone with Avery.

Well, not alone. There was also her phone.

He tried to think of a way to get her attention. Avery always loved complaining about Scarlet in her texts, even though they seemed like best friends on the surface. Finally, he said, "Do you think there could be any more nauseating couple on earth?"

Avery looked up from her phone, her eyes following Rob and Scarlet as they went back into the school. She wrinkled her nose. "Seriously! Oh my God, she talks about him nonstop when it's just us and he's not around!"

"Really," he said, stretching out on the curb and crossing his legs at the ankle. "Rob isn't much better. And did you see their Instagram photos?"

Scarlet had done an entire series of about fifty photos of her and Rob, holding hands, staring at each other, making out. "Yeah. Yeech. Gross. Some things are better kept out of the public eye."

"A lot of things, actually." James smiled when Avery got the hint and slipped her phone into her pocket. "Yeah. So how are things?"

"Oh, you know," she said with a shrug. "Pretty good. It's been awesome with my parents apart. I don't have to listen to them arguing twenty-four-seven. I wish they'd finally just get that and decide that they want to uncouple."

James frowned. "It's not so bad, though, if they decide to stay together. Right? Otherwise, they might uncouple and then realize later that it was a big mistake. And then it'd be too late. Even if you got remarried, you already told that person once before you didn't want to be with them. So, it wouldn't be the same."

Avery stared at him. It was only then that he realized he was droning on, stream-of-consciousness.

"What are you talking about?" she finally said. "Espousing sucks. Always. Uncoupling is the normal thing to do."

He swallowed. "Yeah."

"Are your parents still ..."

"Yeah. I don't know. They act like the best of friends now. Like they're married. I caught them holding hands yesterday. And did you know he stayed over five of the last six nights? In separate bedrooms, of course. But I'm confused. What's that about?"

Avery's eyes widened. "Really? Oh, geez. I'm sorry."

James raked his hands through his hair. "It's not so bad."

She gave him a look that said, *Yes, it is.*

His chest tightened. Why had he told her that? So that he could look even more pathetic? He'd come over here hoping to make her see how cool he was, and now he felt like an idiot. James shook his head. "Forget it. I've got to go."

He stood and headed into the school without another word.

CHAPTER 35

Passion Test

DR. REED SAT AT HER DESK, waiting for the Healys to arrive and reading over her notes from the last session. She had been seeing them every two weeks during their trial separation, viewing the changes in their relationship and how each was handling the separation together … and separately.

Let's see what we have for them today, thought Dr. Reed. Last time, she had told them to do one or more healthy uncouple activities. It seemed that Sara was much more successful than poor Tom. Sara had completed multiple healthy uncouple activities: shopping, writing, exercising, going out with friends. While Tom's only activity was thinking about Sara doing all the healthy uncouple activities, which was *not* a healthy uncouple activity.

A couple of more sessions, and Dr. Reed would write up her report for the court. She hoped she could get a handle on what to recommend for the Healys. Espouse or uncouple?

Today, Dr. Reed was going to concentrate on seeing how much passion, or lack thereof, was left in the relationship. She pulled out an article by a well-known uncoupling therapist. Dr. Reed had adjusted some of the verbiage and looked over her list of *Passion-Less Signs to Uncouple*:

- Burping, farting, and scratching your butt in front of your partner is standard daily behavior.
- Overhearing a conversation about oral sex at the gym reminds you that your annual dental cleaning is overdue.
- The poodle you have been rubbing for the last twenty minutes turns out to be your husband's back.
- According to your wife, the highlight of lovemaking has become the popping sound your hip makes.
- The last time your bed squeaked was when the kids used it as a trampoline.
- Your husband is president of the Scarlett Johansson/Gabrielle Union/Jennifer Lopez fan clubs.
- Your wife is president of the George Clooney/Idris Elba/Chris Hemsworth fan clubs.
- The "steamy" email you sent your husband contained the words: sweatpants, antifungal, Ace bandage, bloating, and fiber-rich.
- You caught your husband eating your edible underwear … out of the box … and instead of being upset, you asked if he could share some with you.
- While giving your wife a massage, you replace the exotic body oil with Pam cooking spray.

Dr. Reed looked over her list. *Yup, that should do it. If they hit about 50 to 60 percent of this list, my recommendation will be to uncouple.*

A knock on the door caused Dr. Reed to rise from her chair with, "Come on in." *I'm interested to see what Sara and Tom will think about this new assignment!*

As the Healy couple walked into Dr. Reed's office, they headed directly for the couch. *Hmm*, Dr. Reed thought to herself, *Getting comfortable with the routine, although not as clingy as they used to be. Well, maybe not as nervous about the sessions anymore?*

As the couple sat, Sara looked intently at her phone. "Oh wow! Unbelievable …"

"What? Are the kids okay?" asked Tom, with concern in his voice.

Sara rolled her eyes at Tom. "It's not the kids. I just got a news alert saying that Matt Damon is getting espoused!"

Tom gave Sara a look like she was crazy. "What? Are you sure you don't mean Ben Affleck? He's the one who is always messing up."

Dr. Reed watched the interaction from her cozy chair while writing notes in her pad.

"I know the difference between the two," quipped Sara, and then quickly deepened her voice. "What is Treadstone? Who is Jason Bourne? I want to espouse." Then she straightened her back and put her hands on her hips. Disguising her voice again, with a slightly different tone, she croaked, "Arrr, go fuck yourself! I'm going to uncouple."

Tom nodded with a smile and a laugh. "Okay, I believe you. Well, at least we are following the example of the good guy!"

Sara looked over at Tom with an air of confidence and stated, "Please. Everyone knows that Jennifer Garner would never have espoused. Too much of a good girl."

Dr. Reed picked up on the lull between them, having enjoyed the interaction, and decided to direct the conversation back to the session. "So, how have you two been doing since we last met? At that session, we discussed the uncouple activities ... and, um, Sara, you seemed to conquer those quite well!" Dr. Reed looked over at Tom, "And Tom, you seemed to do okay ... just need a little more practice, but all-in-all you both seemed to do well."

Sara quickly spoke up. "I guess that means I won!"

Tom's head looked as if it would swivel off his head, so Dr. Reed quickly interjected, "Okay, so that's not how uncouple therapy works."

Sara gave out a laugh, "I know. Just joking ..."

Although, Dr. Reed was not so sure Sara was joking. Tom looked like a hurt puppy dog. She'd better get this on track again. Dr. Reed handed both Tom and Sara a copy of the "Passion-Less Signs to Uncouple" and waited for them both to read it over.

Sara seemed to be amused by the list, as she smiled and giggled, while Tom seemed profoundly serious and disapproving.

"This list is not all-encompassing, but it is always good to get the conversation started ..." Dr. Reed began.

Tom had been squirming on the couch, scrunching up his face. He looked like he wanted to say something and finally blurted, "Okay, all right, I'll go first. Sara doesn't think I'm very romantic. Okay, I said it ..." and he looked over at Sara triumphantly.

Sara rolled her eyes and stated with calm exasperation, "He wears a fanny pack to bed."

"It's for HOLDING SNACKS, SARA!" Tom said, defending his honor as best as possible.

Dr. Reed wasn't sure where to look but did her best not to burst into laughter. "All right, we've decided to start our own list. Great ... um, but why don't we just stick with my list first ... we could always add to it later." She sat back and scribbled on her pad. *Now we are getting to the fun part of therapy.*

"Tom, since you started, why don't we see what Sara has to say?" Dr. Reed sat back comfortably in her chair and flipped to a new page on her yellow memo pad, pen at the ready.

CHAPTER 36

Cold War

THE MOMENT SHE JUMPED INTO THE CAR, Anaya knew something was wrong with her mom.

Usually, Riya would be waiting outside the car, greet Anaya and open the back door to let her in. She'd play a radio station with cheesy nineties pop songs Anaya had never heard of, drum her fingers on the steering wheel, and pepper her with questions about her day as they drove home.

But this time, Riya was inside the car. She hadn't even opened the locks so that Anaya could get in—Anaya ended up jiggling the door handle before Riya remembered. Riya didn't turn the radio on and stayed silent the entire ride home.

"Are you okay, Mom?" Anaya asked as they drove into their neighborhood.

Riya sighed. "Oh, yes. Just thinking about work. One of my patients had some bad test results, so I'm going to be back on a busier schedule."

"Oh. Okay." Anaya frowned. Her mother tried to shield her from her work, but Anaya knew she was probably talking about Dennis Stevens, the man she'd been caring for over the past year. He was the husband of one of the lawyers her dad worked with at court. Over the years, she'd heard an awful lot of her parents' talk wafting up through the venting ducts. Though she had to admit, her parents didn't seem to talk all that much anymore.

But Anaya also didn't think her mother's nursing schedule was all that was on her mind.

She'd heard her father mention something about uncoupling papers. Anaya didn't know what the exact process of uncoupling was, but she knew there were these papers that needed to be filled out and submitted. There had been loud disagreements about signing or not signing or forgetting to sign ... something about signing! At one point, Anaya had dared to hope that her father was dragging his feet because he didn't want to go through with it.

But last night, she'd heard her father say that the papers were all taken care of, all the *i*'s were dotted, *t*'s crossed. There was nothing to stand in the way of their uncoupling now.

Anaya hadn't told anyone, but when she heard that, she'd cried until she fell asleep.

Who could I tell? Her once-best-friend Avery's parents were in the midst of espousing, and Avery behaved like her whole world was coming to an end. Anaya didn't get it, but there were a lot of things she didn't get about Avery these days. James's parents were happily uncoupled, and he seemed to be doing well, as most kids did when their parents uncoupled. Maybe Anaya should just let it go, since it was the natural order of things.

But if it was the natural order, what was going on with her parents?

"Is Dad going to be home for dinner?" Anaya asked as they drove past rows of condominiums. She loved this neighborhood. It had a walking trail, a pool, and a pond with ducks. In another few months, she'd only be living here part-time. Her father's new place was a small, three-bedroom ranch in Greenlawn. They had looked at houses two years ago as a family. They had all had a great time, and she couldn't figure out what had changed.

Riya shrugged. "I really don't know."

That was another thing. The two of them used to know exactly where the other was and when they'd be home, and they would do errands for each other and make sure the other was all right. Now, they barely communicated at all. When they were together, it seemed they were walking on eggshells. The home used to be filled with laughter, with love.

Anaya now wished she could just stay at school. She hated the cold war. She was forever waiting for one of her parents to do something to hurt the other's feelings.

She thought that maybe, if she could get them together, they could talk it out and come to some understanding. Realize that they were better together.

"Well, where is he?" she asked. "Maybe if you two talked ..."

Riya blinked out of her daze to look at her daughter in the rear-view mirror. "Anaya, honey. We say everything that needs to be said. Everything is fine."

CHAPTER 37

Please God ... No

GWEN HELD HER HUSBAND'S HAND TIGHTLY as they waited in the examination room for Dr. Patel. *Funny,* she thought, *just a few months ago, we sat in this room while Dennis was told how well the treatment was working. Dennis had hugged me, and our son had been overjoyed that Dennis had been given another lease on life.*

Who knew that the lease would be so short? How unfair was that? That was like God giving them something precious and amazing, only to say *Sorry, made a mistake!* and snatching it back.

The PET scan had located another tumor in his liver, and this one was aggressive, spreading into his pelvis. Gwen had talked to Riya about all of this as it was going on, and she knew that Riya was dealing with problems of her own, but even so, Riya's words were more alarming than assuring.

"I wish I could say it was good," she'd said somberly. "Just ... pray. Pray, and hope the doctor has another plan. No sense worrying until you know what you're worrying about."

"Would you be able to resume your schedule, should we need you?" Gwen had asked.

"Yes. Of course. Don't give that another thought."

The worst part of it was that Dennis knew. Dennis understood everything that was happening, and while Gwen felt like she was falling apart, Dennis was the one keeping her glued together. He was upbeat, almost carefree. Taking care of her instead of the other way around.

Gwen knew it was a mask. A façade he put on because he didn't want her to worry about him. It broke her heart.

As they sat there watching television, there was a news story saying last year's numbers were in, and it was official—the number of espouses last year had exceeded the number of uncouplings.

"Don't you feel good," Dennis said, patting her knee. "Now you and your clients are in the majority. Business will be good for you if this continues!"

"Numbers aren't the only thing that matters," she sighed. "There'll always be discrimination and shame attached to being espoused."

Dennis nodded. "How are things going with the Healys?"

Gwen smiled at him. Oh, he'd have had a long career, probably as one of those old curmudgeon types who worked until he was ninety, if his body had given him the ability. But now he simply listened in on her cases. "Fine. They're being model clients. Their hearing is in another six weeks, and I don't see any problems."

Dennis nodded. "Good. Good. Carly's not getting on your case?"

She frowned at the use of his ex's name. "Hasn't been. But she has a knack for doing that. We'll see what happens at the trial."

He smiled. "Of all the women I know, you're the only one who could put up with it. You're a strong lady, Sport."

Swallowing, Gwen fought back tears as the door opened and Dr. Patel strode in, grim-faced as ever.

He closed the door, shook their hands, and said, "I know you're both very anxious, so I won't keep you waiting. Unfortunately, the cancer has spread to the surrounding bones in Dennis's hips and spine, which is causing compression of the spinal cord. That was the pain and numbness you've been feeling in your legs, Dennis."

Gwen stole a look at her husband, who was still smiling, though his smile was just a shadow. "What are our next steps, Doc? Another clinical trial? Chemo?"

Dr. Patel shook his head. "I'm afraid there aren't any next steps. We can treat metastasis when it's in the bone, but with the spinal compression, it becomes trickier. It's very advanced, and any surgery or treatment we provide would weaken you too much, never mind the incredible pain and suffering. There's nothing that can be done. I'm so very sorry."

Gwen could not believe what she was hearing. She wanted to scream at the doctor, *Nothing that could be done?* How dare he say these words? He was a doctor, he wasn't supposed to say those things, he was supposed to have an answer. Gwen couldn't cry, speak, or move. She just sat there, staring at the doctor but not really seeing him. The only thing that brought her back was when Dennis grabbed her hand. She looked at him. He seemed strong, resigned. His voice never wavered when he said, "And how long do I have?"

"I won't put a time on it. But you should get all your things in order over the coming weeks," he stated sadly, putting his hands on his desk and leaning toward Gwen and Dennis to look at them more directly.

"Do what you'd like, see who you can, but eventually, the cancer will spread, so both of you and Terrell need to be prepared. If Ms. Passud will continue with in-home care, we'll communicate the care plan to her. I have a social worker outside who will go through all the details. I'm so very, very sorry."

The doctor stepped from the room and closed the door.

Gwen's mind whirled. There were so many people to tell. Terrell, of course. Friends and family. *The coming weeks? A month or two?* Why, that meant he wouldn't even see the summer. His favorite season. They'd talked about renting a house in the Hamptons. *And what about finally taking that trip to Boston in the fall to visit Terrell and meet his girlfriend?* All these thoughts whirled through her mind in a frenzy, none of them sticking.

"Well, Sport," Dennis said to her, putting both his hands over hers, "Looks like I've made my final play."

It was only when the social worker walked in that Gwen realized she did not have the energy or even the desire to move. Gwen covered her face with her hands and allowed herself to cry.

CHAPTER 38

Month Six—The Trial

GWEN SAT AT THE TABLE in the courtroom, forcing her mind onto the Healy case, where it belonged.

They are depending on you, Gwen. They have been waiting long enough. Put your mind on it for just the next hour—the next twenty minutes—and get this done.

Gwen took a deep breath and scanned the room. No wonder it was so stuffy in here—she had never seen the courtroom so packed. She was not sure how or when they'd arrived, but suddenly, she was aware of the chatter.

Next to her, Sara Healy fidgeted nervously, firing off questions, wondering how the proceedings would go. Gwen usually did her best to make sure the questions were answered before her client thought to ask them, but she'd come in here woefully underprepared and hadn't done much to help inform the Healys and set them at ease. Guilt pressed in on her, weighing her down even more.

Tom had pulled out his wallet and taken out two pictures of his children—Sam and Avery. The children who, up to this point, Gwen had only known on paper.

They are not just names on a paper now. They are human beings, and they're depending on you. Concentrate.

Gwen looked to the front of the courtroom where Kadir was standing. He gave her a slight smile, no doubt having heard the worst from Riya. Riya was home with Dennis full-time, where she should be. Riya had told Gwen that she still needed to continue with life, but Gwen felt terrible doing so when Dennis was losing his. Everything seemed so unimportant.

It had been six weeks since the doctor had told them there was nothing to be done about Dennis's cancer. Since then, his health had steadily declined. Four weeks after the visit to the doctor, Dennis could no longer get out of bed, just as the doctor had spelled it out. After that precipitous change, things seemed to fall apart more slowly. One day he wouldn't eat, a few days later, a catheter was needed, and more tubes and bags were added. Now, Dennis was on a steady morphine drip to keep him comfortable. He kept up his positive attitude as much as possible, but he was becoming a shadow of himself. Slowly wasting away.

"All stand," said Vanessa, the bailiff.

Gwen rose robotically to her feet as Judge Abraham appeared in the door, stomping her way up to the bench, wearing her usual frown. When the judge sat down, Gwen collapsed into her chair as if her knees could not hold her up. Kadir handed the judge the documents for the case.

"In the matter of case 200135, Tom and Sara Healy v The State of New York," she announced. "Will the defense please begin?"

"Yes, Your Honor," Gwen said, rising to her feet again. She began lethargically to address the facts of the case, going through each piece of documentation necessary. "The Healys have been model defendants under the scrutiny of this court, adhering to every direction to the letter of the law. They've maintained separate domiciles, the children have lived with each parent according to the parenting schedules set forth by this court, and they have been attending mandated uncoupling counseling. Therefore ..."

Suddenly, she heard a noise coming from the table. A slight vibration.

Her phone.

It broke her concentration enough that she stumbled over a word. No more than that. She was used to ignoring her phone.

But now, she couldn't.

She took a step forward as she said, "Therefore I urge the court to—"

She stopped short when she saw Riya's name appear on her phone. A second later, the phone stopped buzzing. Everyone froze in the courtroom as she reached for her phone, then whipped her head around as she saw Kadir going for his own phone.

"Ms. Stevens, are we interrupting something?" the judge snapped.

"No, I—" She swallowed as Kadir held up his phone and mouthed, *You need to call home.* "Well, yes. Your Honor, may I request a recess of five minutes for a phone call? It's an emergency."

The judge stared at her in disgust. "You're stalling."

"No, actually," Kadir broke in softly, staring at his phone. "She's—"

Judge Abraham silenced him with a savage look. "No recess. We just started. Now, proceed with your case, Ms.—"

"I'm sorry." Gwen walked over to where Kadir was sitting and glanced at the screen of his phone as he held it out to her. *Get Gwen. Tell her to come home immediately.* Gwen turned and approached the judge, trying to quell the churning in her stomach. "But Your Honor, I have a personal matter that needs immediate attention. I am sorry for the inconvenience."

Judge Abraham narrowed her eyes. "You need to check on a personal matter? Now? In the middle of this case?" She let out a snort of laughter. "What you mean is, you are not prepared. Correct?"

"No. What it really means is I have to go," Gwen said, returning to the defendant's table and reaching for her briefcase to pile her belongings inside while trying to keep her emotions in check. *Just need to get out of here. Need to get home.*

As Gwen's back was turned, she heard Judge Abrahams's tongue cluck. "Fine. Then I deny your clients' case to be espoused."

Gwen whirled, noting the stunned looks on her clients' faces. "What?"

The judge stared down at Gwen, eyes glistening. "I believe there may be collusion between the spouses and you as their lawyer to go against the rules set forth by this court. Using this personal emergency is just a stalling technique."

Gwen could not think. She could not see anything but bright starbursts of anger in her vision. Grabbing her briefcase off the desk, she stalked up to the bench. "*You* are a despicable woman, Carly Abraham. You have nothing but hatred and a big black heart in your body. I know your hatred of me is because you uncoupled from my husband. If you loved each other so much, why didn't you fight to espouse? Why did you let him go? Huh? So, now you take it out on everyone."

Judge Abraham's voice was quiet, but everyone could tell she was trying to control her response to Gwen. "I'll remind you that this is my courtroom. Do you want to be held in contempt?"

Gwen was vaguely aware of everyone staring at her, of Kadir pleading with his eyes for her to remain calm, but she didn't care. She was finally saying what she always knew about the judge. And she had more to say.

"I'll tell you why you uncoupled," Gwen seethed. "He couldn't wait to uncouple from a cold, cruel witch like you. That's why. Who in their right mind would want to stay with you?"

The look on Judge Abraham's face—pure shock—would have been a triumph on its own if Gwen wasn't feeling so frantic about Dennis.

She whirled to the Healys. "I'm sorry. I really must go."

Judge Abraham jumped to her feet. "Ms. Stevens!"

Gwen didn't turn around as she continued to stuff her things into her bag. As she turned to leave, she said vehemently to the judge, "For the last time, it's *Mrs.* Stevens."

Sara's eyes widened. "Wait, is that it? We're not espoused?" she began, peppering Gwen with questions as the judge began banging her gavel to get Gwen's attention.

"You stay in this courtroom, Ms. Stevens! You are forbidden to leave! Bailiff!" she screamed, standing up and waving her hands. "If you leave, so help me God, I will throw out this case, hold you in contempt, and make sure no one wants to hire you as their attorney!"

Vanessa began to advance, on course to meet Gwen at the double doors of the courtroom.

Gwen turned, thrust her chin in the air, and said, "I'm going to be by my husband's side, and not you or all the armies of the world can stop me. He's dying, and I'm going to be by his side to make sure he knows how much I love him. Something that people who are in love do for each other. Something you would never have done for him."

Gwen swung around and walked briskly toward the door. Every eye in the courtroom was on her; heads were swinging to the aisle to watch her departure. She eyed the bailiff carefully, hoping Vanessa would not stop her, but Vanessa simply threw open the door and held it to let her pass, uttering a soft, "You go, girl."

As soon as Gwen hit the hallway, she called home. She lifted the phone to her ear as she broke into a run.

Inside the room, the judge sat in stunned silence, a puckered scowl on her face while she tried to remain regal.

The only movement in the room was Kadir, who had decided to follow Gwen and was walking out after her.

"And where do you think you're going?" the judge snapped. "I haven't adjourned this case yet."

Kadir turned. "To support a friend and her sick husband. You know what to do, Judge. Adjourn the case."

He proceeded to walk out of the courtroom without another word from the judge. For the first time in her life, Judge Carly Abraham had been silenced.

CHAPTER 39

Boys!

"LOOK AT THIS," Scarlet said to Avery, who was reaching into her locker to pull out her books for the next period.

Avery groaned inside. Every time Scarlet said *Look at this*, she was talking about something new she had received from one of the parents, or some cool Instagram response she received from one of her followers, or an amazing gift Rob had given her to show how special she was. Avery could not take it anymore. Her mom had told her that just because it was on Facebook didn't mean it was true, and likely, someone who posted her entire life on Snapchat or Instagram was just screaming out for attention. She had said that Scarlet sounded insecure and sad, and Avery should pity her.

Avery wished she could summon pity for the girl. But Scarlet's life was too darn perfect. Avery's mother had bought her front-row tickets for Shawn Mendes this past weekend, for God's sake. The only pity she could summon was for herself since she'd been wanting to go to that concert since literally ... forever.

Scarlet thrust her phone under Avery's nose, making it impossible not to look. It was a selfie she'd posted on her Instagram, cheek-to-cheek with ... none other than the immortal singer himself.

Avery's jaw dropped.

Scarlet even looked great in the picture. *Ugh!* It was too much to ask that she'd snapped a picture with him and ended up looking like a buffalo in it.

"Wow, that's awesome," she bit out, trying to keep the jealousy under control.

"Yeah, he was super cool," Scarlet said, leaning against the locker beside Avery and sighing. "I was going to try to get backstage after the concert, but Mom said no because we had to get back home to relieve the babysitter. So, what'd you do this weekend?"

Avery tried to keep calm. She lifted her books to her chest and wondered how she could make going to the hardware store with her mom and Sam to get stuff for the new garden sound exciting. Other than that, she'd just read the new *People*, watched random YouTube videos, and texted with James. Once. He'd asked her what the math homework was, and she'd told him.

Well, that was something ... she could embellish it.

"Oh, you know, James and I texted all weekend."

Scarlet rolled her eyes. "You've been doing that all year."

Avery sighed. She knew that. It was hopeless. Ever since their last exchange a few weeks ago, when he'd gotten up and left her without a word, he'd been silent. When they'd been together since then, James usually stayed quiet and at a safe distance, except for when Avery coaxed him into a selfie. That's why she'd coaxed him into about a hundred selfies over the weeks—she wanted him to get closer. But he still hadn't gotten the picture. It was pretty clear by now that he wasn't interested. "So?"

"Well, when is he going to ... move things forward?"

Avery sighed again. If only she knew. There was slow, and there was glacial. And now, finally, she understood: There was James's speed, which was *never-gonna-happen*. Dead. No motion whatsoever.

"Speak of the devil," Scarlet said.

Avery whirled to see James coming toward her, Rob by his side. James looked especially good today. He had gotten a haircut, and his hair was shaved on the sides and longer on top. His eyes were trained right on Avery, which made her stomach flutter.

Scarlet reached for Rob, but he held his hands up. "Yo. What's with that picture of you and that guy on Instagram?"

Scarlet laughed at him. "It's Shawn Mendes?"

"I don't care who he is! I don't know why you're taking pictures with him and posting them all over Instagram!"

The two of them began to argue, completely ignoring James and Avery. James gave Avery a little raise of the eyebrows, and the two of them quietly extricated themselves from the fray, walking slowly down the hall toward Avery's next class.

Avery's stomach was still flip-flopping. Alone with James. For the first time in a month. "So," she said, "how was your weekend?"

He shrugged. "'S okay."

Great. Scintillating conversation. She wished she knew just what to say to make things all right between them. Maybe she needed to be flirty and, *blech*, more like Scarlet. She opened up her mouth, thinking *What Would Scarlet Say?* when suddenly, James said, "Hey, I should apologize to you. For running off on you a while back and kinda ignoring you as I have been. It's not you. I've just been going through some weird stuff."

Avery's eyes widened. "What?"

She turned to him. There was pain in his eyes. "Yeah. It's just ... the situation with my parents is confusing. And I don't know what to make of it."

"It's gotten worse?" Avery asked gently, feeling a warmth settle over her. James was talking to her. Pouring out his heart. She could listen to him all day.

He nodded. "They're acting like they're espoused. But they're not. How embarrassing! I think my parents are having an affair!"

Avery was dumbstruck. "WHAT? Wow! I can't believe it! I'm so sorry!" Then she turned pensive. "I kinda understand."

James stuck his pencil behind his ear and shoved his hands deep into the pockets of his jeans. "You do?"

Avery nodded. "My parents are in court right now. My parents will be officially espoused, and my brother and I will officially be weirdos! Although they have been behaving like they are uncoupled ... I thought they would call the whole thing off? I'm confused too!"

The corner of his mouth curved up into a smile. "Huh. I don't get it. Why is it so hard for adults to admit if they love each other or if they want to move on?"

Avery shrugged. "It's not that easy to admit how you feel when you're fourteen, either."

He smiled at her just as Scarlet stormed past them, a look of complete rage on her face. She pushed open the door to the restroom, and it slammed against the pink tile wall before swinging closed.

Surprised, they both looked the other way for Rob. He stalked past them, all red-faced. "I've had enough of her. We're over."

Avery and James shared a wide-eyed look.

"I wonder if she'll be putting that on Instagram?" James said.

Avery burst out laughing.

CHAPTER 40

Dennis

RIYA CHECKED THE IV DRIP AGAIN as Dennis's tall, handsome son, Terrell, sat on a chair at his father's bedside, head on the mattress, shoulders slumped. He was holding his dad's hand in both of his own.

"Where is your mother?" Dennis gurgled weakly.

Terrell raised his head. "She'll be here soon, Pop."

Dennis nodded weakly in understanding. "Did I ever tell you, son, how your mother and I met?"

Terrell smiled broadly. "Yeah, Dad. Many, many times."

A grin appeared on Dennis's chapped lips, framed in white stubble. "I've been so happy. I'm so proud of you and the man you've become. And I have so much love for your mom. She's an amazing woman."

Terrell squeezed his hand, tears misting up his eyes. "Dad. Stop talking. Save your strength for Mom."

Riya got some petroleum jelly and wiped it over Dennis's lips. He didn't seem to notice her there. She put a hand on Terrell's shoulder. She had known the time was getting closer and had spent the past few nights at the house, sleeping in an upstairs bedroom, checking on Dennis every few hours. Riya wanted to help Gwen and Terrell as much as she wanted to help Dennis. Dennis was asleep more than he was awake, he had a difficult time concentrating, and his breathing was becoming shallower. Riya knew she had to contact Gwen as Dennis asked for more and more morphine for the pain. Before he went into a morphine sleep, she knew she had to get Gwen home.

Riya let out a breath of relief as the front door opened. A moment later, Gwen appeared in the door, breathing hard.

"Thank God," Terrell breathed, moving aside to let Gwen take his seat.

Gwen quickly reached for Dennis's hand and looked to Riya. Riya whispered, "I had to increase the morphine."

Gwen's eyes drifted to Dennis. His chest rose and fell ever so slightly, and his eyes were closed. "Is he alert?"

"He was a moment ago," Riya said, then whispered to Terrell, "Let's go on out and give them some time alone."

Terrell nodded, head drooping, and the two went outside. Gwen had called him yesterday, when she felt Dennis had changed, and not for the better, overnight. Terrell had dropped everything at his job and drove the five hours to New York, arriving in his suit at nearly midnight. He had stayed up with his dad all night and now looked haggard, wearing just his white dress shirt, unbuttoned at the throat, and dress slacks. Riya told him she would make him some tea, and he nodded thankfully.

In the bedroom, Gwen gripped her husband's hand and listened to his raspy breaths, wondering if he knew she was there. "Dennis," she said softly. "I'm here, baby."

His eyes fluttered open and settled on her. His voice was just a breath. "My beautiful bride. You made it. I knew you would, Sport."

She smiled. "Are you kidding? Not even an army of judges would have kept me from you." Gwen wished she had not listened to him about going to court for the Healy case. Dennis had insisted, saying he wanted to be there when she came back victorious. Well, she might not have won in court, but she had won the best man in the world.

Dennis let out a slow, labored laugh. "I love you, Sport."

"I love you, too," Gwen said, as the tears she'd held back suddenly started to overflow. "And I want you to know that I learned something. I know that all this uncoupling and espousing doesn't matter. We would have found each other no matter what. There's no way this love could have been stopped."

Dennis stroked the top of her hand with the pad of his thumb. "That's right, Sport."

"I have so much to say to you. For us to still talk about," Gwen said softly, wiping the tears from her face. "I'm not sure, but did I ever apologize to you for being so rude when we first met? I was so suspicious of you. Why would this smart, handsome, kind man speak to me?"

Dennis opened his eyes and, through stammered breaths, said, "I …… remember … I can be … as stubborn …… as you …… too." Dennis's eyes closed again as he tried to get his breath back.

"Well, I'm sorry for being rude. And I'm glad you were so stubborn. These have been the best years of my life … you have been the best thing in my life." Gwen choked back more tears.

Dennis opened his eyes and, mustering whatever strength he had,

"Best years …… of … my … life, Sport. Love … you … forever." Gwen noticed Dennis's grimace, so she called for Riya.

Riya entered the room, with Terrell following right behind her.

Riya gave Dennis another shot of morphine and left the room to give Gwen and Terrell their family time. Dennis seemed to go silent. Gwen felt his hand getting colder, heard his breath get shallower and shallower. He was no longer responsive to her touch or words, although she kept talking to him and stroking his hand with hers. Gwen talked about their wedding, Terrell's birth, and family vacations. She couldn't stop herself from talking about all the years they were together. Gwen was so afraid, afraid that if she stopped, Dennis would disappear. She knew Dennis could still hear her and hoped it would bring him as much comfort as it brought herself and, hopefully, Terrell as well.

Terrell sat on the other side of the bed, holding Dennis's other hand, listening to Gwen go down memory lane. Every once in a while, Terrell smiled and corrected some of Gwen's storytelling. Gwen did not know how much time had passed, and she didn't care. She would stay there forever if it would keep Dennis alive. And then, suddenly, Dennis's eyes opened, and he seemed to catch a breath. He looked over at Gwen, and she could see, in that split second, that twinkle in his eyes. Gwen and Terrell stood up and moved closer to Dennis's face. Just as suddenly as he had opened his eyes, they closed.

Dennis took one last breath and released it, his body going slack, the monitors around him suddenly beeping and flashing. Gwen sat back down, covered Dennis's hand with both of her hands, put her face down onto the bed, and softly wept. Terrell walked around the bed to Gwen, knelt beside her, put his arms around his mother, and cried with her.

Riya came quietly into the room and moved quickly to turn off the monitors. She checked for a pulse but knew she wouldn't find one.

Dennis looked so serene. No more pain. She patted his hand and kissed his forehead, as her own tears wet the dear man's face.

At that moment, Riya realized something.

She knew the reason why everything was so wrong in her life and why she and Kadir and Anaya felt so miserable. It was because they were being torn apart. *I don't want to uncouple. I want to espouse.*

Riya wanted to be there for Kadir. And she wanted Kadir to be there for her until the very end. The only problem was Kadir. *Does Kadir want to espouse?* Riya was not too sure.

Wiping the tears from her eyes, she moved the monitors away from the bed to the corner of the room. In the silence, the only sound was the soft, desperate murmur of Gwen's sobbing.

CHAPTER 41

Letting the Barriers Down

RIYA WAS EXHAUSTED. Gwen had been so distraught that Riya had Terrell take his mom to her bedroom while Riya called the funeral home and waited to have Dennis taken from the house. Once Dennis was gone, Riya continued packing up the medical equipment and monitors, stripping the bed, and just trying to figure out what else she could do for Gwen and Terrell. Riya felt terrible. *Grief ... I know it is one of those emotions that a person must move through themselves, but it certainly makes everyone else feel so useless.*

A soft knock made Riya jump. *Who can this be?* She moved quickly to the front door, feeling annoyed and hoping to get there before there was another knock. She opened the door, fully prepared to send whoever it was away, and was shocked to see Kadir. Riya just stared at

Kadir for several seconds before waving him into the house. She could see in Kadir's eyes the pain and sorrow she was feeling.

"How's Gwen?" Kadir asked Riya, speaking very softly.

"So, you know? Dennis is gone," Riya whispered, trying not to break down in tears.

"I could see it in your eyes," Kadir whispered, taking Riya's hands in his own.

Riya caught her breath but stayed strong, not wanting to completely break down. "Gwen is resting in her room. Terrell is with her. Not sure it's such a good time to bother them."

Kadir looked intently at Riya. "I know. It's not why I came. I came to see you. See if you needed any help ... or support. Not that you need me ... but ... I just ..."

Riya interrupted, "Yes, yes, I do need you. And I don't mean here or now ... I mean always. I will need your help ... always."

Kadir breathed in deeply, his eyes darting around the room, the way they always darted around when he wasn't sure of himself or what to say. "I need you too. I need you always."

"Well, I want to espouse. There, I said it. I know you believe we should follow the uncouple laws and do the right thing, but ... I don't want to uncouple. I want what Gwen and Dennis had ... what you and I have now and, I believe, we will have forever ..." Riya's thoughts spilled out all at once, and she thought to herself, *Where is your self-control?*

Kadir brought his hands up to Riya's face and quickly added, "I want to espouse as well. I'm an idiot. After the judge was so cruel to Gwen, then she ran out of the courtroom, and I was rude to the judge ..."

"Wait, what?" Riya said, pulling back from Kadir with concern in her voice. "What happened to Gwen in the courtroom? You were rude to the judge?"

Kadir shook his head. "I'll tell you about it later. It's just that it hit me today that I didn't want to lose you. I want to espouse. And, if the judge fires me because of it … well then, you will just have to work a lot more to support Anaya and me," he finished with a wry grin.

Riya smiled and took Kadir's hands in hers. "I love that you want to espouse, Kadir. I really do, but you need to be sure of what you are saying. Today has been an emotional day, and tomorrow or the next day, you may change your mind."

Kadir's face dropped. "What? I just told you that I want to espouse. My mind won't be changed …"

Riya stopped him. "Kadir. I can't agree to the espouse yet. We have been battling for weeks. I think if we had wanted to espouse, we would have been on the same page from the beginning. I feel so much uncertainty … except for my love for you. But I need to be certain that you want it too."

Riya saw that Kadir was stunned and hurt.

Kadir spoke quietly. "Okay, well, then I will prove to you that we should be together. I will do whatever you want, but I will not change my mind … ever."

"Wait, what time is it?" Riya said, looking at her watch. "Five-thirty! Anaya …"

"I'll pick her up," Kadir replied. "You stay as long as Gwen and Terrell need you. We will be at home waiting for you."

Riya hugged Kadir with her heart full, even though she knew there would be difficult times ahead. *But finally, some hope, hope that he really does want to espouse.*

Kadir headed out the door to pick up Anaya, and Riya headed to Gwen's room. *Gwen and Terrell need to eat. And maybe I can call some friends and relatives for them.*

CHAPTER 42

Can We Get Back to the Healy Case?

JUDGE ABRAHAM SAT IN HER CHAMBERS staring up at the ceiling. Then she looked over at the clock. *Wow. Almost 6 p.m. Time to go home.* It had been a very long day, a large caseload, too many after the Healy case. How did she get through them all after that one?

She could use a big shot of whiskey.

When she was half her age, a practicing attorney on her way up, she used to keep a bottle of JD in her desk, just for days like this.

Didn't this robe mean anything anymore? She'd worked damned hard to get where she was. Since when did a lawyer just run out on her? Insult her? And her own clerk, disobeying her? What the hell was going on in this world?

Clenching and unclenching her fists, she wished she had something to punch. One thing was certain: she wasn't going to let them get away with it. Heads were going to roll. Kadir was fired. Well, maybe not fired, but she certainly would make him think she was going to fire him. And Gwen Stevens? She'd hold her in contempt and throw out her case due to collusion. Let the Healys start all over with a different attorney.

She heard a knock on the door. Judge Abraham thought of pretending she wasn't there. It was late, after all, and few people knew she stayed late to catch up, but perhaps it was Kadir coming to apologize. She'd let him grovel, then give him a "second chance." It would make her feel better. "Come in," she thundered.

The door opened, and Robert Feinstein entered.

She rolled her eyes. Well, here was something to punch, at least. "What do you want?" she snapped.

He closed the door and stood there, fidgeting. She was surprised by how nervous he looked. "I just wanted to ask about the Healy case."

The judge wanted to stab his eyes out with a pencil. "What about it?"

"Well. I need to know. Were you serious about throwing out the case?"

"Yes, what do you think I meant by collusion?" she answered angrily, opening a file on her desk and hunching over it, hoping that he'd get the message she was still in control of this case even though her feelings felt extremely out of control.

Feinstein stood calmly and commented, "I saw no evidence of collusion. I believe they've done everything right."

She nodded. "Is that so? I believe I was right with my decision."

Robert was behaving too calmly and still standing his ground. "Yes, that may be so. At the very least, Judge, you should reschedule. Be fair to the Healys and out of some respect to Mrs. Stevens."

The judge grew angry and threw her hands up. "I don't have to do anything out of respect for anyone. I will be the one to make the final decision."

He nodded, turned around, and put his hand on the doorknob.

"Mr. Feinstein, let me ask you a question. Did you like your wife?"

He stared at Judge Abraham for a moment. Robert walked toward her desk and sat across from her. "Yes, I loved her. But when it came to our uncoupling year, we were more like friends. We'd run our course. Uncoupling was just the natural thing to do."

"And after you were uncoupled a few years, you never missed her?"

Robert put his briefcase on the ground, pulled his ankle to his knee, and thought for a moment. "No. I missed certain things about being with someone. But not her, no."

"Did she remarry?"

Robert nodded. "She did. Two years after we uncoupled. She and her new husband had six kids together. *Six*. Two sets of twins! I could never have handled that!"

The judge's eyes widened. "Didn't you feel like you were missing out on anything? Like they were having a party you weren't invited to?"

"No. Uncoupling was fine with both of us. Maybe it would have been different if we had had kids, but we just went our separate ways. I'm glad she's happy."

The judge took a deep breath. Sitting comfortably in her chair, she swung it slightly from side to side.

"I was married to Ms. Stevens's husband, you know. We uncoupled."

He cleared his throat. "Yes. I might have heard that in the hallways."

"When we first married, I was twenty-five, and we were both just out of NYU Law. We had fun together, so much fun."

Robert was staring at her with a quizzical expression. She could tell he did not believe her.

"It's true! I know how to have fun. At least, I used to. But Dennis liked to take things easy, and I was ambitious. So ambitious, I hardly devoted any time to anything other than my job. I didn't want kids, even though he did. I ignored him, we started living different lives until uncoupling time came, and it was done. It was fine by me." The judge stopped swinging her chair and sat up as if suddenly realizing this fact for the first time.

"But really, we didn't espouse because we no longer loved each other. I don't even believe Dennis would have espoused. I felt we wanted different things. I was not engaged in the relationship. I never gave Dennis a reason to want to espouse. But I never stopped loving Dennis. I dated for a few years, but nothing was close to what I had felt for Dennis. None of them even made the radar screen that he was on."

Judge Abraham rubbed both palms over her face. "Even so, when I look back at my life, I realize that I was incredibly happy with Dennis. I just think, for me, I made the right choice. I am good at my job. I am fiercely independent. I became an espouse judge. It would have been difficult to do that while working on a relationship and raising kids. Kids, ugh! I think what keeps me up at night is—would kids have been so bad? Would being with Dennis have been all worth it? And then I snap back into reality, and I do think I chose the right path and I am fine … more than fine. I'm good."

Robert pressed his lips together. "Some couples do deserve to stay together."

The judge nodded slowly. "I suppose I've been giving Gwen a hard time, but she has always rubbed me the wrong way. Dennis or no

Dennis! Back in the day, couples didn't think about espousing; they just uncoupled. It was so much easier."

Robert Feinstein's phone buzzed, and he looked down to read the text.

"Oh right, rudely look at your phone while we are in the middle of a conversation," the judge drawled sarcastically.

Robert dropped his chin to his neck, then looked up, his face very solemn.

"What?" the judge said abruptly. "What now?"

Robert looked intently at her. "Dennis. It's Dennis, Carly. Kadir sent me a text. Dennis has passed."

Judge Abraham felt like someone had hit her in the face with a tennis ball. That had happened to her once while playing with a male attorney who thought she needed to be put in her place. The pain was so intense that it paralyzed her entire body.

Judge Abraham buried her face in her arms, on her desk, and began to sob.

Robert took a deep breath. He went to the door, made sure it was locked, and came around the judge's desk. He put a hand on her arm. "Carly," he said. "I'm so sorry."

The judge pulled herself together and sat up in her chair, pulling her arm from Robert's hand. She thought of telling him not to be so familiar with her, but right now, she needed to pull herself together.

"We should do something about the Healy case," Robert said, understanding that the judge wanted to get back to familiar territory.

The judge's eyes narrowed. "I don't want to talk about that now. What's wrong with you?"

He shrugged. "Maybe now's the perfect time to talk about this case. Maybe now you can finally be objective about it."

Judge Abraham sighed, then looked at her tear-stained calendar. "Fine. Set up a date two months from now. That should give Ms. Stevens time to grieve her husband and, if need be, find another lawyer to step in for the Healys. I will go over the case again before the new trial, but that is all I am promising. No guarantees. Time for you to leave, Mr. Feinstein."

Robert nodded and did as she said.

When Carly went back to her work, though, she thought of the first time she had met Dennis, in law school. She was sitting in the front row of Principles of Law when a man with a dark, scruffy beard approached her and pointed to the empty seat next to her. "You look like the smartest person in class, so can I sit next to you?" Carly had snapped back at him, "How do you know if I'm the smartest person in the class?" Dennis had smiled that irresistible smile and said, "Well, would you have talked to me if I had said I wanted to sit next to the most beautiful woman in the class?"

Only Dennis could have pulled off that line with her. She smiled at the memory.

He was a good man, and he had deserved to have a good wife who cared for him in the way she'd never been able to.

Dennis had been the only man she had ever loved. She could not believe he was gone. Carly felt heartbroken. She put her arms back on the desk, lowered her head, and cried.

CHAPTER 43

Still Not Espoused

TWO NIGHTS AFTER the fiasco of the trial, the Healys and Baums meet at Meehan's for dinner.

Jessica could not believe what Sara and Tom were telling them about the day in the courtroom. Boy, she and Michael had missed out on one exciting day. It was like a scene out of some TV drama, with the defense attorney yelling, the judge banging her gavel, the defense attorney and judge's clerk both storming out, and everyone in the courtroom completely stunned. It had seemed more like a murder trial than a regular, boring old espouse hearing. It was the main topic of conversation, leaving them all wondering what the heck would happen next.

"Does this mean you guys have to uncouple?" Jessica asked them after they were served coffee. It was a weekday night, tables were full, but they had managed to be seated quickly.

Tom shook his head. "Well, we thought we were done for. But we got a call from Robert Feinstein, and due to our lawyer's personal situation, they're going to grant a new trial in two months."

Sara nodded. "Poor Gwen. Her husband passed away later in the day after the courtroom scene. He had cancer. That's why she ran out."

Jessica clutched at her heart. "Oh! That poor woman. But you will still use her? After that mess?" She looked over at Michael, who had been playing footsie with her under the table, steadily moving his foot up her leg. *Geez, he's like a high school kid again, constantly wanting some.* The last thing she needed was for the Healys to catch wind of it. She kicked him swiftly to put him off.

"Yes, it must've been horrible for her. The judge wasn't very nice at all. Tom and I discussed it, and we like Gwen. It was not her fault. She decided to show up for us, knowing how sick her husband was at home. We feel we should show the same loyalty," Sara said.

"The judge was the first wife of our lawyer's husband—they uncoupled," Tom pointed out.

"What?" the Baums said in unison.

"Yeah," Tom said. Sara could tell Tom loved presenting this little tidbit of gossip. "The bailiff mentioned it to us the first time we were in court."

"Yeah, Gwen said right to the judge 'he never would've espoused you'!" Sara chimed in. "She was always so in control, and then she just exploded! Gwen had never mentioned it to us. How terrible that must have been for her. I don't understand why that was a problem for the judge—most people uncouple."

Tom frowned. "Maybe the judge had wanted to espouse? Maybe that's what her problem is with people getting espoused? I certainly hope that judge will grant us the espouse."

Michael shook his head. "You told us that you followed every espouse rule to the *T*. That judge has to allow you to espouse."

"Right. Right," Tom said slowly, reaching over and squeezing Sara's hand.

"I guess we'll just have to see." Sara lifted her hand from under Tom's and ran it through her hair. "Thank you, guys, though, for being so supportive of us through all this craziness."

Jessica smiled. "Of course, don't thank us."

"Are you kidding? We are friends with the celebrity espouse couple of the town! Uncoupling is not this exciting," Michael teased.

"So," Jessica said, once again swatting Michael under the table. Now he had his hand on her knee. "It seems you guys have been through the ringer with everything you need to do to espouse."

Tom nodded in agreement. "Shitload of paperwork. Uncouple counseling. Child custody schedules. Taxes to be paid, house to get ready to sell. Lots of rules you need to follow. But you know, it'll be worth it in the end."

Just then, the waiter came to refill coffee and see if anyone wanted an after-dinner drink. Michael ordered two Irish coffees for himself and Jessica. Tom ordered one Irish coffee for himself and looked over at Sara as if to say, "Order your own drink."

Sara didn't miss a beat. "I'll take a Sambuca on the rocks. Thank you."

She gave her husband an icy yet triumphant glare.

Michael raised an eyebrow. "You guys don't seem too upset that you're going to have to wait another two months?"

Jessica couldn't help but agree. "Yeah. I have to say, for two people looking to espouse, you guys look really happy to be uncoupled."

The Healys looked at one another, surprised.

Then Tom smiled, his eyes drifting to the space between Michael and Jessica, where Michael was once again trying to squeeze Jessica's knee. "And you two are uncoupled, and yet you're behaving like you're espoused. What's your point?"

The table froze for a couple of beats before everyone burst out laughing.

CHAPTER 44

Last Day of School

ANAYA STOOD IN FRONT OF HER LOCKER, reaching in and pulling out papers, clips, and school notices that had piled up all through the school year. She had taken all her notebooks home during the week after each class final exam, so she just had to clean up all the other useless stuff in her locker. The school allowed the last period on the last day of school as locker clean-out. The school custodian walked down the hall, intermittently placing garbage cans so the kids could empty out the year's worth of stuff from their lockers—which not only included papers, but sneakers, hair bands, brushes, locker mirrors, shirts, shorts, pants, bottles, cans, and the ever-forgotten, lost, moldy lunches.

Anaya was in a good mood. Not only did her school finals go well, but her parents seemed to be on better terms. It was not exactly back to normal, but there weren't the long silences between them, the clipped conversations, or even any fighting, and her father behaved like every day was Mother's Day! He brought her mom flowers, did the wash, cleaned the kitchen after dinner, always asked about her mom's day, and even took the initiative to order dinner during the week. Whatever was going on, it was much better than it was a few weeks ago. Even if this meant they had decided to go through with the uncoupling, well, that was okay. Anaya had come to terms with it. It was the normal thing to do, and if it meant her parents would get along better, then she was all for the uncoupling.

If only Anaya could get her heart to match what her head was telling her.

She looked up to see Ms. Kim, dressed head to toe in bright yellow: bright yellow pants, bright yellow shirt, bright yellow espadrilles, and a bright yellow headband that barely kept her red, curly, frizzy hair under control. Ms. Kim was singing to the tune of Mister Rogers' "A Beautiful Day in the Neighborhood" as she went down the hallway. "It's a beautiful day to clean out our lockers, a beautiful day to clean out our lockers! Won't you be happy, won't you be happy … when you have clean lockers!"

Anaya looked up and down the hallway at the kids "cleaning out" their lockers. Most of them were just hanging around talking. One group was playing basketball using the garbage can. It seemed most of them would never do well at basketball. Anaya had to smile to herself as Ms. Kim pranced by her. *Why is she always so happy? You have to be a little kooky to always be that happy, right?*

Anaya looked across the hall and saw James standing at his locker, but he was not cleaning it out. He was staring further down the hall at something. Anaya strained her neck to see if she could see what he was looking at. *Of course, it's Avery.* Anaya could see Avery standing at

LAST DAY OF SCHOOL

her locker and jabbering away with Scarlet. Occasionally, they would put their heads close together, whisper something, and then burst out laughing, completely oblivious to everyone else. *Oh brother, James, just go over to her already. Ask her out or tell her you like her or whatever boys and girls do when they like one another*, Riya thought. *Geez, they are behaving like my parents!*

Anaya decided she had to do something. If she could not do much about her parents, she could try to do something about Avery and James. She strode over to James's locker, which was still jam-packed with books, papers, and everything else he had thrown in there during the year. Anaya tapped him on the shoulder and said, "Hey James. How's it going?"

James jumped a little, taking him away from his concentration on Avery. "Hey," he said. "Um, going good, how 'bout you?"

Anaya decided to dive right in. James might get upset, but this was the last day of school, so it wasn't like she was going to see him the next day. She went with her best course of action—lie. "Hey, so you and Avery are now a thing, uh?"

"What, no, who told you that?" James quickly shot out.

"Oh, I overheard someone in homeroom class?" said Anaya, trying to think quickly on her feet.

"Who in homeroom?" asked James, a little angrier than Anaya had expected.

"You know, I don't remember, I mean, no one was surprised. Everyone knows you and Avery like each other. You guys are great together," quipped Anaya.

"What? Really, people are saying this? I, uh, um, I, I mean, Avery and I aren't, um ... Do you think Avery likes me?" James stumbled while putting his hands in and out of his pockets. "If she does, well, you know, that's great, but if not … you know, that's um, well, it's great to be friends too, right?"

"What? Friends? Come on, you guys would be the 'it' couple of Oldfield. You know, you would be known as 'JamVery.'" Anaya squirmed after saying that, and looking at James, who was now thoroughly disgusted, thought, *Okay, too much … back it up*! "I mean, yeah, Avery likes you. All she ever talks about is 'James said this, and we talked about that, and James likes such and such.' She never stops … but, please, don't tell her I told you. I mean, if you have not already asked her out or anything … I don't want to cause any problems …"

James seemed to calm down and looked down the hall at Avery again. "Hmm, well, it is the last day of school. Maybe I should talk to her or something?"

"Okay, I'm going to help you out. Let's take a walk down to Avery's locker and just start up a conversation. Hopefully, Scarlet will scatter when you start talking. I will say I have to get back to cleaning my locker. Okay?" Anaya hoped that Scarlet would leave; otherwise, this would become more awkward than it already was.

James hesitated for a few seconds. "Okay. Yeah, I mean, if you want to, I don't want to force you or anything … I can do this … on my own."

Anaya jumped in before James changed his mind. "It's no big deal. We've known each other forever … so act natural." *Not like me*, she thought to herself. Her mind was a jumble, and her nerves not much better. *What am I doing? What if this doesn't work? No, it will be fine. Okay, start moving. James will follow.* And with that, Anaya started walking toward Avery, James moving in step with her.

Anaya could see Avery spot them coming her way. Avery whispered something to Scarlet, who scurried away with a quick peek at Anaya and James.

Just breathe, you got this, Anaya thought. As they reached Avery, Anaya said, "Hey Avery, last day of school. How did your exam—"

"Hey, heard my parents talking last night. Today is the big day for your parents, right? They have their trial to become espoused," James blurted.

Yeah, that's being subtle, thought Anaya. *This is not gonna go well!*

"I just want it to be over. It is going to be weird being in one house … all together again," replied Avery. "I really wish they would uncouple the way normal people do. When are your parents uncoupling, Anaya? It has to be soon?"

Anaya was taken aback slightly. "Um, yeah, real soon. You know, like everyone else … Everything normal."

"Ugh, you are so lucky! Whenever my parents are together, all they do is argue. Why do two people want to stay together when they can't agree on anything?" pondered Avery.

"I think all parents are messed up. My parents are uncoupled, yet we are always together as a family. Every night for dinner, watching TV together, and even planning vacations together. It's weird but also seems okay. I think my parents should have espoused," James confessed.

This was not the way Anaya had thought it would go … she was going to walk up, get Avery and James talking, and slink away. Now, she felt like Ms. Kim, listening to people's confessions … and then she started confessing herself.

"Actually, it's not going normally at my home either," blurted Anaya. "I don't know why I said that. I think my parents are confused. I think they want to espouse, but they are behaving like they are going to uncouple. I know this is weird, but I wish my parents would espouse. I am a nerd. What can I say?"

"No, well, yes, you are a nerd, but not about your parents," Avery said. "So, let me get this straight. I want my parents to uncouple, James would not mind if his parents had espoused, and Anaya would like her parents to espouse, but they do not know what they want. Did I get this right?"

Anaya and James laughed. "Yes, you got it right," Anaya replied.

James straightened, put his hands in his pockets, and with his head slightly tilted, said, "Maybe we should go down to the courthouse and straighten out our parents. We would do a better job than they seem to be doing."

Ms. Kim suddenly appeared next to Anaya with her big smile. "What is happening here? I don't see locker cleaning going on?"

Anaya took Ms. Kim's arm. "You are right. Gotta get back to cleaning. Should we sing something on the way back to my locker?"

Ms. Kim almost jumped out of her skin, she was so excited. "I would love to!" That was all Ms. Kim needed, once again breaking out to the tune of Mister Rogers' beautiful neighborhood. "Summer is here once again! We are all together for one more day. Have a great summer, have a great summer, won't you have a great summmmerrrrr!"

Anaya stole a backward glance to see Avery and James smiling and talking. *Worked out okay. I think when I get home tonight, I'm going to do the same with my parents.* She looked over at Ms. Kim. "Ms. Kim, do you have those espouse counseling sessions over the summer? I may want to join."

CHAPTER 45

Second Time Is a Charm

IT WAS THE LAST DAY OF SCHOOL for the kids and the start of summer for everyone. The courtroom was packed. It seemed everyone in the town of Huntington had heard what had happened the last time this case was in court. Some people came to see a show, but most people were there to support Gwen. Many could not believe Gwen was back so soon, and back for this case. *It was your run-of-the-mill espouse case, give it to someone else, do not allow Judge Abraham to humiliate you again,* had been the advice from friends and family.

Gwen had also been surprised that the Healys still wanted her to represent them after the courtroom fiasco, but they had been very insistent she remain their lawyer. Gwen figured they both thought that the judge would grant them the espouse decree due to her behavior. Well, if that is what they thought, it was fine with Gwen.

The Healys had introduced Gwen to their good friends the Baums, who had come to support them. Gwen also noticed Riya in the crowd. Robert Feinstein sat at the prosecutor table with Dr. Teresa Reed next to him. The courtroom was standing room only, with many lawyers Gwen and Dennis knew, court stenographers, court officers, and security personnel. *Wow!* Gwen was baffled, but she could also feel the love and support from everyone. Dennis would be so pleased!

Gwen could not believe she was in the courtroom so soon either. She had debated about ever setting foot in a courthouse or even whether she would practice law again. A few days before Dennis passed, they had gone back and forth on what she would do when he was gone. Who would she talk to about her cases? What difference did she make in anyone's life? But Dennis had made her promise not to give it up immediately. "Give it a year, Sport. Promise me a year," Dennis pleaded. "And if you hate it, if it doesn't make you happy, then give it up. But you are good at this. Just a year."

Because she believed in love, or at least Dennis believed she did, that was worth fighting for.

Gwen smiled to herself as a thought of them together during younger, more carefree days flitted through her head. When the bailiff told them to stand, she stood, still feeling that warmth in her heart from Dennis. She wondered if he was up there, somewhere, watching her. She knew he would be proud of her.

Judge Abraham entered, her face stone cold as usual. Gwen noticed that she had gotten a haircut, and the color was more of a honey blond, not platinum, with her lips painted a bright red. When she sat, she nodded and said, "Good morning, everyone."

Gwen nearly fell over. Where was Judge Abraham?

"Case number 200135. The case of Tom and Sara Healy v the

State of New York, to become espoused," bellowed the bailiff giving Gwen a wink.

"Your Honor," Gwen began, standing very quickly, wanting to get in the first word. She knew she could easily draw Judge Abraham's wrath this way, but she had something to say. "Please, let me say something."

The judge's lips twisted. "Must I? Did you forget again that this is my courtroom?" But she didn't wait for a response and replied, "Well ... if you must."

Gwen looked over at her clients. Sara was shredding a corner of the notebook page in front of her, and Tom looked as though he had swallowed lye. They were so nervous; it was all her fault. She had to make this right for them. "The Healys have been through so much with this case. It is my fault that it has taken so much longer. I am pleading with the court ... with you, Your Honor, to allow them to espouse. They've done everything according to the rule of the law, and—"

Across the aisle, Robert Feinstein stood, looking as if he wanted to save Gwen and give her support. "Yes, I wholeheartedly agree. The Healys have done everything correctly, my report states as much, and I don't see anything to stand in the way of us granting an espouse decree."

The judge cleared her throat, clearly trying to stay calm. "That may be all well and good, but what I would still like to say is that—"

Suddenly, Gwen detected movement out of the corner of her eye. A voice cried, "I want to uncouple!"

Gwen whirled around to see Tom standing beside her, fists clenched. Everyone stared at him.

He swallowed. "I don't want to espouse. I want to uncouple."

Sara stared at him. "Wait, what? Do you want to uncouple, seriously? After what we have been through the past eight months?"

He nodded, sat down beside her, and turned to face her as he took her hand, ignoring all the people watching them. "Yes. I am sorry. I don't know why I couldn't bring myself to say it before, but I do. I want to uncouple."

Gwen gave him a look of utter disbelief. "Mr. Healy, this is not the time for this! You don't know what you're saying."

"I've just ... I don't know. I am happier. Sara seems happier. The kids are happier. And I may have met someone else, which is new and exciting," Tom said, looking out into the crowd. Sam-the-girl's mother gave him a little wave. "I don't know why we are fighting the norm."

A big smile broke out on Sara's face. "Oh, thank God! It's fine. I agree. In fact, I am so relieved. I do love being uncoupled. For the first time in years, I am making my own decisions, and I'm happy to be working again! We get along better. The kids really are happier going between the two homes, it's ... I'm so happy!"

Gwen watched them, a look of pure disbelief on her face, as the crowd dissolved into murmurs. "Wait. Sara, you feel the same as Tom?"

For the first time ever, the judge shared Gwen's sentiment. She slammed her gavel as the Healys embraced. "Order, please! What the hell is going on here?"

Dr. Reed stood up and exclaimed, "Ah, thank goodness. Ignore my report findings, Your Honor. These two should uncouple. They completely failed my *passion quiz.*"

The judge hit her gavel once more, "STOP. Enough ... passion quiz? Sit down, Dr. Reed."

Everyone looked at the Healys. Tom stood and said, "We would like to—"

"I want to espouse!" a voice blurted. All the heads swung, this time in the direction of the side bench, where Kadir had risen to his feet.

Gwen and the judge both breathed out, "What?" as Kadir strode across the courtroom until he was standing in front of Riya.

Riya's eyes filled with tears. "You are doing this now?"

Kadir grabbed Riya's hands in his. "Yes, now. In front of everyone. I love you. I want to stay married to you. Please tell me you want to espouse me!"

Riya jumped into his arms, "Yes, a million times, yes. I believe you! Let's get espoused!"

Judge Abraham banged her gavel with three hard knocks. "Okay. Everyone. Get control of yourselves. Kadir, this is not your hearing. What are you doing?"

For the first time in a long time, Kadir could not wipe the smile from his face. "Judge. I am sorry, but I don't care if you fire me. I'm okay with that. But I'm going to fight to stay with my wife." He looked at Gwen. "Mrs. Stevens, we want to get espoused. Will you represent us?"

Gwen did not know who to turn to. She was still stunned from the Healys' outburst. "Um, what? Excuse me, but the judge is right. We must get back to the Healy case. Are you sure?"

"Yes, we're sure!" chimed in both Riya and Kadir.

The judge banged her gavel once again. "Great. Nice sentiment, Kadir. Now get your ass where it belongs so we can continue this trial."

I don't even know if there is a trial, Gwen thought, looking at her clients.

Suddenly, someone in the galley jumped up. It was Michael Baum, grabbing Jessica's hand. "As long as we're announcing our intentions, I have something to say. I want to marry my wife, um, I mean, ex-wife. Again. If she will have me. I never should've uncoupled from her."

Jessica jumped up. "Yes, yes, I'll re-marry you!"

They embraced, kissing each other passionately in front of everyone. A few oohs and ahhs were heard around the courtroom.

"Who the hell are you?" an exasperated Judge Abraham blurted.

"Oh, those two are our best friends. They are uncoupled but have been doing a really terrible job at it!" said Sara with a big grin.

Gwen approached the bench, bewildered, but feeling terribly angry. "It's your fault they want to uncouple. You made it too difficult for them to espouse! It's a wonder anyone in this town can get espoused with you making it so impossible!"

The judge gave her a superior glance. "What are you talking about? I was ready to grant the espouse decree!"

Gwen blinked, speechless. *She was?* "You were not, were you?"

Suddenly, Robert Feinstein, who had been watching all this quietly, stood. He said, in a voice loud enough to silence everyone in the room, "Everyone just shut up and settle down!"

The judge and Gwen stopped talking, turning to Robert as the rest of the chatter in the courtroom came to a complete stop.

"I've been watching all of you over the past few months, and I have to say, you've behaved like a bunch of idiots."

The judge shot him a look of disdain. "Now, wait a minute, I'm not—"

"You too, Judge. And for once, please be quiet and let me speak." He stared her down, a challenge in his eyes.

Judge Abraham swallowed her words at once.

He turned to the Healys. "You two want to uncouple?"

They nodded.

"Fine, then do it. Get your paperwork in, but hurry. Your time's almost up. And don't forget to attach the late fee." He turned to Kadir. "It's about time. Really, it is inexcusable that you took this long to tell your wife what you thought. Worried about what the judge would think of you?" He hooked a thumb at Judge Abraham, who appeared too shocked by his taking control of her courtroom to object.

Kadir pressed his lips together, plunged his hands into his pockets, and nodded.

"You love your wife, and you want to be with her forever. So, get it done."

Gwen smiled at Riya. "Well, that's the truth."

Robert looked at her. "Quiet, now," he said gently. "I'm not done."

He next turned to the Baums. "And you two ... I don't know who you are, but if you want to re-marry or espouse instead of uncoupling, you've got a mess on your hands—legal fees, taxes, selling your second home, parental schedules—and I definitely see uncoupling counseling." He glanced over at Dr. Reed. "But hire Gwen. She's the best espouse lawyer in the business."

Michael and Jessica nodded. Michael shyly spoke. "Thank you. Ah, we will."

The judge once again cleared her throat. "Mr. Feinstein. I admire what you're trying to do, but I remind you, this is still my courtroom."

Robert turned to her with an unapologetic look on his face and strode toward the bench. "I know that, Judge. But I am not done yet. I still have something to say to you."

"Is that so?"

"Yeah. If you'll pardon me, for just another moment longer."

Judge Abraham's eyes widened, and her mouth opened and closed.

"Now, I admire you a lot because you are one tough woman, you're a fantastic judge, and you don't let anyone get the better of you. In fact, I more than admire you. I would like to ask you on a date, but you make it so difficult."

Every eye clung to the woman in black on the bench. The judge's nostrils flared, her fists balled, and every person in the courtroom held their breath, waiting for her to blow her top. They waited for Robert Feinstein to be kicked so hard up the backside that they would have to peel him off the ceiling.

But her expression melted away to quiet confusion. "Did you just say you wanted to ask me on a date? In my courtroom? In front of all these people?"

He nodded thoughtfully. "I believe so."

For the first time, Judge Abraham began to stumble over her words. Her face pinked. "Date? I'm no spring chicken."

"Neither am I, in case you didn't notice," Robert said. "And didn't I just get done telling you that you should be nicer to people who want to be together? I want to be *with you*."

Everyone in the courtroom held a collective breath.

And then suddenly, miraculously, something happened.

Judge Abraham smiled.

Not a smile of triumph over revenge, or the evil smile that she sometimes had when one of her foes suffered a misfortune. No, this was entirely different. It seemed like happiness, and it transformed her entire face.

Finally, she answered, more sternly, "I will answer the question another time."

He winked at her. "Don't take too long, Carly."

She grabbed her gavel and banged it. "This is still my courtroom, and I can still hold all of you in contempt!" she shouted angrily while staring at Robert.

He nodded, apologized "to the court," and went back to his table.

Tucking a lock of honey-blond hair behind her ear, Judge Abraham summoned her composure and looked at the defendants. "First, I must adjourn this case. Mistrial on the basis that one and/or both persons involved in the espouse trial want to uncouple." She looked at Riya and then spoke to Kadir. "Hire yourself a lawyer. I think we both know who that will be. If you believe you belong together, then get it legally done right."

The Passuds nodded.

Then Judge Abraham swung her gavel once more. "This courtroom is adjourned. No espouse decree. Let the uncoupling begin."

Judge Abraham turned to Gwen, who had walked slowly back to her chair, sat down dejectedly, and stared into space, seeming not to know what to do.

"Counselor," the judge said to Gwen, "I'll see you in my chambers."

CHAPTER 46

No Uncouple Law?

GWEN STEVENS HAD NEVER BEEN in Judge Carly Abraham's chambers. A couple of months ago, she had been certain this was where the judge kept her pitchfork, devil horns, and the souls of the people who'd crossed her.

But the office was simple, well-kept, and homey. The judge had potted plants, her NYU Law diploma on the wall, and personal photographs of her and famous people she had met, like Ed Bloomberg, Hillary Clinton, and President Bush. Gwen's eyes widened and misted over when she saw a picture of Judge Abraham, from her younger days, with a much younger version of Dennis in a dark scruffy beard.

Gwen smiled.

Maybe Gwen was beginning to understand Judge Abraham a little more now. It had started at Dennis's wake. Judge Abraham came, greeted everyone in the family politely, and sat quietly at the funeral parlor for hours, wiping her eyes occasionally, staring at Dennis's coffin. She had sent the largest flower arrangement. And at the funeral, Judge Abraham quietly sat in the back of the church, and Gwen noticed her at the cemetery watching the proceeding from a distance.

As Judge Abraham removed her robe and sat, Gwen said flatly, "So, you won. The Healys are going to uncouple after all. Congratulations."

The judge shrugged. "You and I both know that it's what they want. Otherwise, they might have gone a year into being espoused and found out they would rather be apart. And that would've been a bigger mess."

Gwen nodded, conceding. "I suppose."

"Still, I was not very easy to work with. And I never will be, but I do promise not to be a double bitch to you." The judge leaned forward as if getting ready to impart a great secret. "Have I made myself clear?"

Gwen stood there, hardly able to hear the words. *What? Clear? What does that mean? Is this a Judge Abraham apology?*

Before Gwen could reply, the judge continued, "I am sorry for blaming you for Dennis and I uncoupling. It was the right thing for us to do. We were not meant to be together forever. The uncoupling law worked the way it was supposed to with us."

Of course, Gwen thought, *the uncoupling law worked the way it was 'supposed to.' A half-assed apology. Well, better than no apology at all.*

"I appreciate your sentiments and hope we can do better when working together," Gwen half-spat.

"Working together? I am a judge who upholds the law for uncoupling. You are a lawyer for people who want to espouse. Not sure working together will ever be easy," said the judge, more sternly.

"Geez, can you never put your work aside for one moment?" Gwen said with as much control as she could muster, while thinking, *Keep your cool. I think she is trying.*

The judge's eyes grew dark and intense. She seemed to be ready to raise the stakes and prove who was the boss.

Then she stopped herself, took a breath, and confessed, "I am very sorry for Dennis's passing. He was truly a wonderful man."

A smile almost broke out on Gwen's face, but it was subdued. "Thank you. I appreciate that and accept your apologies," she said. After a beat of silence, she added, "Does this mean we can become friends?"

The judge cringed. "Don't push your luck! You still believe in all that mushy stuff, but I sure as hell do not. Look, I still need to do my job, and you need to do yours. I will play by the rules, and you will need to make sure you are doing your job for your clients."

They both sat awkwardly for a minute, and then Gwen said, "Okay. I can live with that."

The judge smiled, then nodded her head. "I can live with that too."

They were still sitting quietly when the door opened. Robert and Kadir entered the chambers.

"Hmm, no blood. Good sign," Kadir said under his breath to Robert.

"It's good to see you two getting along," Robert teased.

The judge waved him off. "I've heard enough from both of you today. I really don't want to hear anything espouse for the rest of the day."

"Well, over 50 percent of the country is getting espoused today. Who would have ever predicted it would get so high?" Kadir pointed out.

Gwen smiled. "Over fifty percent. It's crazy," she said pensively. "I was thinking about that last night. Can you imagine what it would be like if the law were reversed?"

Judge Abraham raised an eyebrow. "What do you mean?"

Kadir chimed in, "Oh, so … if the law was, once married, you stayed married unless you wanted to uncouple?"

Gwen nodded. "Yes. Imagine if there were no laws that said you had to uncouple after fifteen years. You had to stay together after being legally wed until you wanted to separate. You uncoupled if you no longer loved each other or wanted to be together."

They all thought about that for a moment.

Robert scratched at his temple. "What would a thing like that even be called?"

Gwen shrugged. Kadir pulled out his phone and started to type in Google search. Gwen continued, "There would be no second home investment, no uncouple taxes, but people would battle over property and any other assets, and, what about the kids? Would the court have to decide the visitation, or do the kids decide? It sounds uncivil."

Judge Abraham shook her head. "It would never work! One person in the marriage who disliked the other, wanting to get away from that person, would certainly make for a he said/she said fight. Who would leave the home … and where would they go? It would be more than uncivil. It would be a mess. And what if you met someone else and knew you could not get out of the marriage? Would you sneak behind the other person's back?"

Robert added, "Doesn't sound like I would have a job? No need for a state prosecutor. The couple would probably hire their own attorneys. That's expensive!"

"Oh for crying out loud," the judge said. "It would be terrible. People pitting themselves against one another instead of working together. Well, now saying it out loud. It may be more fun to watch people fighting with each other across the aisle."

Gwen spoke up. "Maybe it wouldn't be so bad. Why should the couples who want to stay together have to go to court to do so?"

The judge and Feinstein looked at Gwen and then at each other and laughed.

Kadir read from his phone. "Divorce. It means to make or keep separate or a separation between things that were or ought not to be connected. Sounds like a word that would apply to that situation."

The four of them silently mouthed the word, thinking on it some more. All together, they started laughing. Ridiculous! Unthinkable! Then Judge Abraham clapped her hands. "Okay, if we're done here, all of you, out! I believe I have a date tonight." She cocked an eyebrow at Robert. "Unless you changed your mind?"

"Heck no!" Robert said, momentarily caught off-guard. He straightened his tie, smoothing it down on his chest. "I'm free!"

On those words, Gwen stood up and said to the judge, "See you in court, Your Honor."

Judge Abraham shot back with a red-lipped smirk. "See *you* in court, *Mrs.* Stevens."

Gwen smiled and walked out with Kadir. They strolled arm in arm down the hallway.

"Divorce," said Gwen, eyeing Kadir. "I don't think that's such a bad way to go. I think I wouldn't mind helping people who wanted to end a bad marriage."

Kadir looked surprised. "I don't know. It would seem there would be a lot of acrimony, hurt, and fighting. It seems so much nicer to have a team, two people, working on a relationship they believe in. Why do you think that?"

Gwen shrugged. "Although I do believe Dennis and I would have wound up together no matter which way the law fell, if the law had been different, and I had been a divorce lawyer, and I happened to represent Dennis … I would have kicked the judge's butt!"

Kadir laughed, "Ah, now the underlying truth comes out! Revenge!"

"Well, Kadir, for now, that's not how it works," Gwen said, patting his arm. "I guess we'd better get to work on your espouse proceedings?"

Kadir nodded. "Yep. And let us hope Judge Gardner is back from heart surgery soon. I hear there is this other judge who is a real pain-in-the-ass when it comes to espouse cases!"

They both laughed as they walked out into the warm summer afternoon. It was a perfect day for espousing, for uncoupling, for whatever made people happy. It had not been the most orthodox day the courtroom had ever seen, but it had been a good one, nonetheless.

Gwen thought of Dennis and smiled; he would have loved today's results.

It had been a victory for relationships, for family, for love.

The End

Acknowledgments:

THANK YOU to the My Word Publishing team who helped me through the process of creating this book. Special thanks to owner/ founder of My Word Publishing, Polly Letofsky, for her guidance, enthusiasm, and expertise as my publishing manager. To the amazing Alexandra O'Connell, editor extraordinaire, for taking my inconsistent babble and turning it into a coherent, consistent, fun read. To the talented designer, Victoria Wolf, for making it all look beautiful (like a real book!).

To all my friends and family who, over the past couple of years, always asked, "How is the book going?" —your belief that I would get this done always helped propel me forward. Special thanks to Beth Ann, Michael, Patrick, Megan, Susannah, Wendy, Margaret, Diane, Sharon, Jason, Maria, the Donahoe cousins, Lois, Jennifer, and Patty. And last but not least, to my two children—Katlin and Colin—the first two I think about when waking in the morning and the last two I think about when going to bed.

About the Author

JEAN MARIE DAVIS was born and raised in Huntington, New York. After graduating from Southern Illinois University—Carbondale, she moved back to Long Island, where she worked in the marketing research industry for over thirty years. She currently lives in Centerport, New York, close to her daughter and son.

Made in the USA
Middletown, DE
23 July 2021